POKÉMON ADVENTURES: DIAMOND AND PEARL/ PLATINUM
Volume 9
VIZ Kids Edition

Story by HIDENORI KUSAKA
Art by SATOSHI YAMAMOTO

Translation/Tetsuichiro Miyaki
English Adaptation/Bryant Turnage
Touch-up & Lettering/Annaliese Christman
Design/Yukiko Whitley
Editor/Annette Roman

Printed in the U.S.A.

Published by VIZ Media, LLC
P.O. Box 77010
San Francisco, CA 94107

10 9 8 7 6 5 4 3 2 1
First printing, October 2013

www.vizkids.com

www.viz.com

Art
Satoshi Yamamoto

Pokémon
Adventures
Diamond and Pearl
Platinum
Story
Hidenori Kusaka

Our Story So Far...

Lady

Dia

Pearl

A STORY ABOUT YOUNG PEOPLE ENTRUSTED WITH POKÉDEXES BY THE WORLD'S LEADING POKÉMON RESEARCHERS. TOGETHER WITH THEIR POKÉMON, THEY TRAVEL, BATTLE, AND EVOLVE!

SOME PLACE IN SOME TIME... THE DAY HAS COME FOR A YOUNG LADY, THE ONLY DAUGHTER OF THE BERLITZ FAMILY, THE WEALTHIEST IN THE SINNOH REGION, TO EMBARK ON A JOURNEY. IN ORDER TO MAKE A SPECIAL EMBLEM BEARING HER FAMILY CREST, SHE MUST PERSONALLY FIND AND GATHER THE MATERIALS AT THE PEAK OF MT. CORONET. SHE SETS OUT ON HER JOURNEY WITH THE INTENTION OF MEETING UP WITH TWO BODYGUARDS ASSIGNED TO ESCORT HER.

MEANWHILE, POKÉMON TRAINERS PEARL AND DIAMOND, WHO DREAM OF BECOMING STAND-UP COMEDIANS, ENTER A COMEDY CONTEST IN JUBILIFE AND WIN THE SPECIAL MERIT AWARD. BUT THEIR PRIZE OF AN ALL-EXPENSES PAID TRIP GETS SWITCHED WITH THE CONTRACT FOR LADY'S BODYGUARDS!

THUS PEARL AND DIAMOND THINK LADY IS THEIR TOUR GUIDE, AND LADY THINKS THEY ARE HER BODYGUARDS! DESPITE THE CASES OF MISTAKEN IDENTITY, THE TRIO TRAVEL TOGETHER QUITE HAPPILY THROUGH THE VAST COUNTRYSIDE.

Maylene

VEILSTONE CITY'S GYM LEADER, WHO SPECIALIZES IN FIGHTING-TYPE POKÉMON.

Fantina

HEARTHOME CITY'S GYM LEADER, KNOWN AS THE ALLURING SOULFUL DANCER

Gardenia

ETERNA CITY'S GYM LEADER, WHO SPECIALIZES IN GRASS-TYPES.

Professor Rowan

A LEADING RESEARCHER OF POKÉMON EVOLUTION. HE CAN BE QUITE INTIMIDATING!

Saturn

HE IS IN CHARGE OF THE BOMB AND RARELY STEPS ONTO THE BATTLEFIELD HIMSELF.

Mars

A TEAM GALACTIC LEADER. HER PERSONALITY IS HARD TO PIN DOWN.

Volkner

SUNYSHORE CITY'S GYM LEADER. A LONER WHO SPECIALIZES IN ELECTRIC-TYPE POKÉMON.

Candice

SNOWPOINT CITY'S GYM LEADER. A POWERFUL GYM LEADER WHO SPECIALIZES IN ICE-TYPE POKÉMON!

THE TWO BODYGUARDS TASKED WITH ESCORTING LADY SET OUT TO CATCH UP WITH DIA, PEARL AND LADY. BUT THEY LOSE THEIR TRAIL WHEN THEY GET MIXED UP IN THE SUSPICIOUS ACTIVITIES OF MYSTERIOUS TEAM GALACTIC, WHO ARE BUSILY CREATING TROUBLE IN THE SINNOH REGION. DIA AND PEARL FINALLY REVEAL TO LADY THAT THEY ARE NOT HER REAL BODYGUARDS, AND ALTHOUGH IT SHAKES HER UP FOR A MOMENT, LADY RESOLVES TO STICK WITH HER FRIENDS AND TRUST THEM AGAIN.

WHEN CYRUS PERFORMS HIS RITUAL AT SPEAR PILLAR, THE TWO POKÉMON OF THE SINNOH LEGEND, DIALGA AND PALKIA, APPEAR! USING THE POWER OF THE "RED CHAIN," CYRUS ORDERS THE TWO POKÉMON TO BEGIN AN EPIC BATTLE! THIS BATTLE CAUSES TIME AND SPACE TO BE DISTORTED. THE MOMENT FOR A FINAL BATTLE TO SAVE THE WORLD HAS ARRIVED, BUT THE GYM LEADERS HAVE ALL BEEN DEFEATED! WILL PEARL, DIA AND PLATINUM BE ABLE TO STOP THIS CATASTROPHE...?!

Cyrus

TEAM GALACTIC'S BOSS. AN OVERBEARING, INTENSE MAN.

?

AN EERIE SCIENTIST IN CHARGE OF THE RESEARCH AT TEAM GALACTIC.

Sird

A MYSTERIOUS BEING WHO APPEARS OUT OF NOWHERE. SHE SEEMS TO BE A MEMBER OF TEAM GALACTIC... BUT IS SHE REALLY?!

Jupiter

A BATTLE-LOVING TEAM GALACTIC LEADER WHO DEPLOYS POWERFUL ATTACKS.

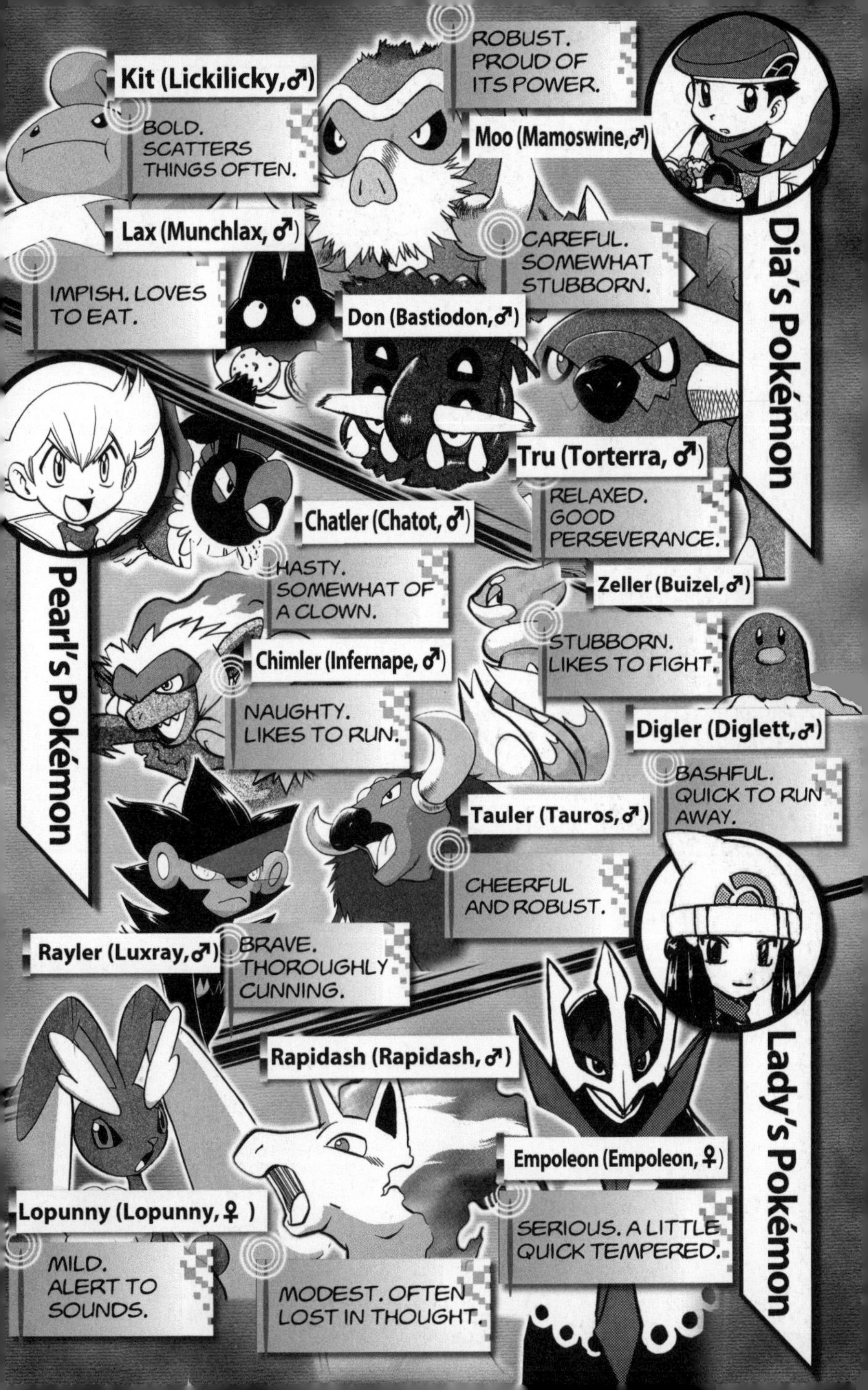
Dia's Pokémon
Kit (Lickilicky, ♂)
BOLD. SCATTERS THINGS OFTEN.
ROBUST. PROUD OF ITS POWER.
Moo (Mamoswine, ♂)
Lax (Munchlax, ♂)
IMPISH. LOVES TO EAT.
CAREFUL. SOMEWHAT STUBBORN.
Don (Bastiodon, ♂)
Tru (Torterra, ♂)
RELAXED. GOOD PERSEVERANCE.
Pearl's Pokémon
Chatler (Chatot, ♂)
HASTY. SOMEWHAT OF A CLOWN.
Zeller (Buizel, ♂)
STUBBORN. LIKES TO FIGHT.
Chimler (Infernape, ♂)
NAUGHTY. LIKES TO RUN.
Digler (Diglett, ♂)
BASHFUL. QUICK TO RUN AWAY.
Tauler (Tauros, ♂)
CHEERFUL AND ROBUST.
Rayler (Luxray, ♂)
BRAVE. THOROUGHLY CUNNING.
Lady's Pokémon
Rapidash (Rapidash, ♂)
Empoleon (Empoleon, ♀)
SERIOUS. A LITTLE QUICK TEMPERED.
Lopunny (Lopunny, ♀)
MILD. ALERT TO SOUNDS.
MODEST. OFTEN LOST IN THOUGHT.

Pokémon Adventures Diamond and Pearl Platinum

CONTENTS

DIAMOND PEARL

PLATINUM

Double Trouble with Dialga and Palkia III

THUMP
GO, MOO!!
THUMP
THUMP
SO THAT'S DIA'S NEW POKÉMON...
..A MAMOSWINE!!
HE ONLY JUST POPPED OUT OF THE POKÉ BALL...
...BUT I CAN ALREADY FEEL AN INTENSE CHILL ALL THE WAY FROM HERE!!
KA-THUMP

SCHNIK
THE ATTACK WORKED!! MAMO-SWINE'S TUSK MUST BE MADE OF ICE!!
AND THOSE TWO LOOK TO BE DRAGON-TYPE POKÉMON !!
ICE-TYPE AGAINST DRAGON-TYPE! THAT'S AN EFFECTIVE ATTACK, DIA!!
DO IT AGAIN, MOO !!
WOOSH
TING
THUMP
THUMP THUMP

SHINK
HUH?
WHAT HAPPENED?!
KA
FWUMP
THAT ATTACK JUST RIPPED THROUGH... THE SPACE...DIA AND MOO WERE IN!!

WOW... AN ATTACK THAT TEARS THROUGH SPACE!!
BUT I GUESS WE'D BETTER NOT CELEBRATE TOO EARLY JUST BECAUSE WE STRUCK OUR TARGET...
WE'VE GOT TO JOIN IN THE BATTLE OUR-SELVES!
ZELLER!
BOM
DIGLER!!
BOM
TAULER!!
BOM
USE THE COMBO ATTACK WE'VE BEEN WORKING ON!!
SHWNK
DIG
DIG
DIG
DIG
TILT
BUMP

KRASH
THUD
FOOSH
FWSH
FWSHFWSH

NOW'S OUR CHANCE, MOO!!
GWUSSH
KRACK-
KRACK
SHHHOOO
TING
WAY TO GO!!

ROOAAR

KNUSH
GID GID
GIDGID
IT REVERSED THE FLOW OF TIME WITH ITS ATTACK!!
FWASSH
AAAAH!!
KER-SCRAPE

THEY'RE STRONG!! ALMOST TOO STRONG!!
THEY'RE NOT CALLED LEGENDARY POKÉMON FOR NOTHING!
AND LIKE CYNTHIA SAID...
...THEY'RE THE ONES CREATING THE DISTORTION IN TIME AND SPACE.
SO BY STOPPING **THESE** TWO, WE CAN SAVE THE SINNOH REGION FROM...
...CATASTROPHE.
WILL WE DEFEAT THEM...?
OR CAPTURE THEM...?

EITHER WAY, WE'VE GOT TO DO IT ON OUR OWN!!
FWIP FWIP
PEARL !!
DIA-MOND !!

DIALGA AND PALKIA ARE A DUO OF TIME AND SPACE...
SO IT'S DUO AGAINST DUO!!
PULL
STRETTCH

WHUP
FLASH
SHO NK SH UNK SHUNK
TH DO NK
KE RSM AK
KRMB
KRM
BL
OH MY ...
I MUST DO MY BEST AS WELL ...
I'M NOT GOING TO LET THOSE TWO FIGHT ALONE!!

IT'S...
...GYM LEADERS!!
...THE...
THEN...
DID THOSE TWO POKÉ-MON DO THIS?
THEY'RE WOUNDED!
I ASSUME SO.
...PEARL AND DIAMOND MIGHT GET HURT TOO!!

PLA... TINUM?
CAN-DICE!!
YOU'RE FINALLY HERE... WHAT TOOK YOU SO LONG?
I WANTED TO SHOW UP ALL COOL AND COL-LECTED...
BUT I'VE ENDED UP LIKE THIS— IN TATTERS.
I WAS THINKING OF GIVING YOU...
...THIS FROSLASS SO WE COULD FIGHT TOGETHER.
I'LL...
...ENTRUST THIS CHERRIM TO YOU.
I DON'T HAVE MUCH OF ANYTHING TO GIVE YOU...
BUT... TAKE THIS.
VOLKNER WANTED YOU TO HAVE IT...
HER TEAM SHOULD BE A LITTLE BETTER OFF WITH THAT.

YOU SURE ARE GOOD AT MAKING FRIENDS, YOU KNOW...
THANK YOU VERY MUCH!
I PROMISE TO REPAY YOU ALL FOR YOUR GENEROSITY!
LOOK OUT!!
SMASH
THE POKÉ BALLS!!

HOW COULD YOU?! HOW DARE YOU TREAT GYM LEADERS LIKE THAT?!
WAIT!! YOU CAN'T GO INTO BATTLE WITHOUT A PLAN!!
BUT...
FWUSSSH
AAAH !!
BOOOM
KLATTR
HUH ?
THIS IS AN ANCIENT SCROLL, ISN'T IT?
AND THESE ARE... ANCIENT WORDS.
ROAR OF TIME...
SPACIAL REND...

CAN YOU READ THIS, PLATINUM?!
YES, I CAN.
THIS HAS BEEN PASSED DOWN FOR GENERA-TIONS IN MY HOMETOWN. MY GRAND-MOTHER GAVE IT TO ME.
I'M HOPING THIS WRITING WILL TELL US SOMETHING ABOUT DIALGA AND PALKIA...
YOU KNOW...
COME TO THINK OF IT, CYRUS DID SAY...
IF I CONNECT THIS WITH WHAT WAS WRITTEN IN THAT DOCU-MENT...
YEAH...
CYRUS MUST HAVE READ THIS SOMEHOW TOO.
BUT... YOU'VE REALLY SUR-PRISED ME.
CYN-THIA...
DECIPHERING THIS DOCUMENT MIGHT HELP US FIND A WAY TO STOP THOSE TWO POKÉMON!
YES!!
I HAVE TO FIND A WAY TO DISCERN ITS MEANING!!

THE ONE WHO CALLED THEM ...
...IS CYRUS.
THOSE TWO POKÉMON WERE SUMMONED HERE BY THE RED CHAIN TO FIGHT EACH OTHER...
IT LOOKS LIKE WE'VE STILL GOT A CHANCE! BUT... THERE'S ANOTHER QUESTION THAT REMAINS UNANSWERED...
BUT HE'S NOWHERE TO BE SEEN!
WHERE IS HE...?!

ADVENTURE MAP
DIAMOND
Spear Pillar
TRU
Torterra ♂
KIT
Lickilicky ♂
LAX
Munchlax ♂
MOO
Mamoswine ♂
DON
Shieldon ♂
PEARL
Spear Pillar
CHIMLER
Infernape ♂
ZELLER
Buizel ♂
CHATLER
Chatot ♂
TAULER
Tauros ♂
RAYLER
Luxray ♂
DIGLER
Diglett ♂
PLATINUM
Spear Pillar
EMPOLEON
Empoleon ♀
LOPUNNY
Lopunny ♀
RAPIDASH
Rapidash ♂
Oreburgh VS Roark Coal Badge
Eterna VS Gardenia Forest Badge
Veilstone VS Maylene Cobble Badge
Pastoria VS Wake Fen Badge
Hearthome VS Fantina Relic Badge
Canalave VS Byron Mine Badge
Snowpoint City VS Candice Icicle Badge
Sunyshore City VS Volker Beacon Badge

77
Double Trouble with Dialga and Palkia IV

ROAR OF TIME ...
SPACIAL REND...
THESE MUST BE THE MOVES PEARL AND DIAMOND WERE ATTACKED WITH!!
PALKIA USED SPACIAL REND TO TEAR AWAY SPACE.
AND DIALGA USED ROAR OF TIME TO REVERSE THE FLOW OF TIME.
ROOOAR
DID YOU SEE THAT, DIA?
LADY AND CYNTHIA ARE READING SOME KIND OF SCROLL.
EYEP!

MAYBE THEY'LL FIND A SOLUTION TO ALL THIS. IN FACT...
I **KNOW** THEY WILL!
I'M SURE LADY WILL FIND IT!!
THOSE TWO FOCUSED THEIR ATTENTION ON US THE MOMENT WE GOT HERE...
DOES THAT MEAN THEY DON'T WANT TO FIGHT EACH OTHER ANY-MORE?
OR IS IT THAT ...
...THEY NO LONGER HAVE A **REASON** TO FIGHT?
COULD IT BE THAT THE ONE WHO WAS COMMAND-ING THEM TO BATTLE IS NO LONGER HERE?
AND DOES THAT MEAN THAT... CYRUS IS GONE?!
Such fools ...

CYRUS'S VOICE!!
WHERE IS HE?!
It will engulf every-thing.
WHAT ?!
The new core will engulf every-thing.
It will...
RMBL RMBL RMBL
... spread and engulf ...
...all that is incom-plete.

KRASH!
EVERY-THING!!
PEARL!! DIA-MOND!!
THUMP
ARE YOU OKAY?!
I'M FINE.
I WANT YOU TO KEEP WORKING ON DECIPHER-ING THAT SCROLL, LADY.

NO DOUBT ABOUT IT—THAT WAS CYRUS!
ISN'T THAT RIGHT, DIA?
DIA ...?
BLRMBLRM
THERE'S NO NEED FOR ME TO GIVE THEM ORDERS ANY-MORE...
THE CREATION OF A NEW UNIVERSE CAN NO LONGER BE HALTED.

SMASH
BOOM KRASH
THE DISTORTION IS GETTING WORSE.
YOU WERE A LOT STRONGER THAN THE GYM LEADERS DURING THAT POKÉMON BATTLE, JUPITER.
YOU WERE ...
...MORE AFFECTED BY THE DISTORTION THAN THEY WERE.
BUT THEY WERE DISORIENTED WHEREAS YOU REMAINED CALM.
SO YOU SHOULDN'T BE EMBARRASSED ABOUT LOSING. AS A MATTER OF FACT, YOU SHOULD BE PROUD.
HEH HEH HEH HEH...
HMM ...
AS IF THAT'S GOING TO COMFORT HER...
WHO IS THIS WOMAN ANYWAY, JUPITER?

TEAM ROCKET MEMBER SIRD, ONE OF THE THREE BEASTS.
ACTU-ALLY...
...TEAM GALACTIC MEMBER SIRD.
I'M ONE OF YOUR COMRADES. I JOINED TEAM ROCKET FOR A REASON.
COMMANDER CYRUS'S PLAN TO CREATE A NEW UNIVERSE WAS ALREADY SET IN MOTION YEARS AGO.
YOU TWO KNOW THAT, DON'T YOU?
THAT'S RIGHT...
WE WERE CAPTURING POKÉMON WHO HAD A CONNECTION TO THE STARS AND THE COSMOS.
CLE-FAIRY.
LUNA-TONE.
STARMIE.
SOLROCK.
STARYU.
CLEFFA.
THERE ARE MANY POKÉMON CONNECTED TO THE STARS AND THE COSMOS...
...BUT THERE IS ONE POKÉMON WHOSE POWER EXCEEDS THEM ALL...
I DISCOVERED A POKÉMON WHO REPRESENTS THE POWER OF THE UNIVERSE ITSELF. ITS NAME IS...

...DEOXYS!
GIOVANNI, THE LEADER OF TEAM ROCKET, WAS TRYING TO CAPTURE DEOXYS.
AS SOON AS I FOUND OUT ABOUT IT, I JOINED TEAM ROCKET— AS A SPY.
PRETENDED TO PAY ALLEGIANCE TO GIOVANNI.
BUT MY SOLE MOTIVE WAS TO PRESENT DEOXYS TO COMMANDER CYRUS.
I LEARNED QUITE A BIT WHILE INSIDE TEAM ROCKET...
I AM SIRD OF TEAM GALACTIC ...
AT TIMES, I LEND A HELPING HAND TO THOSE I BELIEVE ARE JUST TOO GOOD TO FADE AWAY... HEH HEH HEH HEH...
BUT YOU WERE STOPPED JUST WHEN YOU WERE ABOUT TO GET YOUR HANDS ON DEOXYS!
ISN'T THAT RIGHT ?!
YES ...

BECAUSE OF THOSE BLASTED ...
...KIDS WITH POKÉ-DEXES!
MY LEFT LEG WAS STRUCK BY A SPECIAL ICE ATTACK DURING THAT BATTLE.
TCH... I CAN'T MOVE.
I'LL HAVE TO CALL MY COMRADES IN SINNOH FOR HELP.
HEH HEH HEH... BUT I'VE MADE SOME INTERESTING DISCOVERIES ALONG THE WAY.
THE PETRIFAC-TION OF HUMANS ...
THAT DISCOVERY ALONE MAKES UP FOR THE INJURIES I'VE INCURRED.
THE MOMENT I TRIED TO CAPTURE DEOXYS WHILE TRYING TO ESCAPE...

AN UNEXPECTED EFFECT WAS CREATED WHEN MEWTWO'S ATTACK...
...CLASHED WITH AN ATTACK FROM MY POKÉMON!

I'LL GO AFTER DEOXYS, ENTITY TWO, AS WELL AS INVESTIGATE THE MECHANISM OF THIS PETRIFACTION.
THIS IS NOT THE MISSION I WAS GIVEN... BUT I KNOW ITS IMPORTANCE WILL SOON BECOME APPARENT.
AND SO, WHEN THE GRUNTS CAME TO RESCUE ME...
I WON'T BE ABLE TO RETURN TO SINNOH FOR QUITE SOME TIME.
I NEED SOME-ONE TO TAKE MY PLACE WHILE I'M GONE.
I'LL HAVE **YOU** STAND IN FOR ME.
THE TEAM GALACTIC GRUNTS ARE CONTROLLED BY A GROUP CONSCIOUSNESS. THEY MOVE TOGETHER AS ONE IN PERFECT SYNCHRONICITY.
BUT I PURPOSELY FREED ONE OF THEM FROM THAT MODE AND INSTILLED MY OWN CONSCIOUSNESS IN HIM.
THIS IS THAT GRUNT.
I FOUND HIM BURIED UNDER THE RUBBLE OF THE VEILSTONE CITY BUILDING AND BROUGHT HIM WITH ME.

IN SOME WAYS, THIS FELLOW IS MY ALTER EGO.
HE WILL MOVE, THINK AND BEHAVE EXACTLY AS I WOULD.
AND WHAT HAPPENED TO DEOXYS?
WELL ...
I HAD HEARD THERE WAS A GRUNT WHO SUCKED UP TO COMMANDER CYRUS ALL THE TIME...
...SO IT WAS **HIM**, HUH?!
RIDICULOUS.
HEH HEH HEH HEH ...
I WAS ATTACKED BY MEWTWO WHILE GOING AFTER DEOXYS.
MEWTWO HAD BECOME FRIENDS WITH THOSE POKÉMON TRAINERS. IT MUST HAVE WANTED TO FREE THEM FROM THEIR PETRIFACTION.
TO BE HONEST, IT WAS A NARROW ESCAPE TO RETURN HERE.
YOUR WORK IS OVER. THANK YOU FOR YOUR SERVICE.

I NEVER EXPECTED HIM TO GET SO OBSESSED WITH THOSE POKÉDEXES...
BUT RECEIVING THEM IS QUITE A BONUS!
SO THAT'S HOW THIS ALL FITS TOGETHER ...

WHO ARE YOU?!
RILEY FROM IRON ISLAND!
LUCARIO, CLOSE COMBAT!!
FSSSSHH
BDUMM
THAT'S THE GUY WHO WAS SPYING ON DIA, ISN'T IT?
BUT ...
...WHEN I TRIED TO FIND OUT WHO SENT THIS SPY CAMERA ...
...I SENSED... SOME-ONE ELSE.
THE DIS-TINCT PRES-ENCE OF AN EVIL AURA ...
... THAT WASN'T HIS.

...IT WAS YOURS!!
AURA SPHERE !!
WHISH
WHISH
WHISH
WHISH
FFT
FFT
FFT
FFT
FFT
I'LL TAKE CARE OF HIM.

YOU CAN'T STOP IT ANYMORE!
ZUKK
ALL THAT IS INCOMPLETE WILL BE SUCKED INTO IT.
THE CORE WILL SWALLOW EVERY-THING.
IT WILL SPREAD AND ENGULF ALL EXISTENCE.
THAT WHICH IS FAR AWAY WILL COME CLOSE. THE PAST WILL BECOME THE PRESENT.
THE DISTORTION OF TIME AND SPACE WILL SPREAD EVER FASTER AND THIS INCOMPLETE WORLD WILL COME TO...
...AN END.

ADVENTURE MAP
DIAMOND
Spear Pillar
TRU
Torterra ♂
KIT
Lickilicky ♂
LAX
Munchlax ♂
MOO
Mamoswine ♂
DON
Shieldon ♂
PEARL
Spear Pillar
CHIMLER
Infernape ♂
ZELLER
Buizel ♂
CHATLER
Chatot ♂
TAULER
Tauros ♂
RAYLER
Luxray ♂
DIGLER
Diglett ♂
PLATINUM
Spear Pillar
EMPOLEON
Empoleon ♀
LOPUNNY
Lopunny ♀
RAPIDASH
Rapidash ♂
Oreburgh
VS Roark
Coal Badge
Eterna
VS Gardenia
Forest Badge
Veilstone
VS Maylene
Cobble Badge
Pastoria
VS Wake
Fen Badge
Hearthome
VS Fantina
Relic Badge
Canalave
VS Byron
Mine Badge
Snowpoint City
VS Candice
Icicle Badge
Sunyshore City
VS Volker
Beacon Badge

78

Double Trouble with Dialga and Palkia V

FLOWER SHO
WHAT?!
IMPOSSIBLE!!
HUH? WHAT?
IT'S REAL!!
THE DISTORTION IN SPACE AND TIME...
...JUST LIKE CYRUS SAID...IT'S SPREADING!!

COME ON— SPILL IT!
SINNOH POLICE STATION
WHERE DID THE TEAM GALACTIC GRUNTS AT THE GALACTIC VEILSTONE BUILDING DISAPPEAR TO?! YOU KNOW, DON'T YOU?!
WE DON'T! REALLY, WE DON'T!
WE JUST FOLLOWED ORDERS TO CLOSE OFF LAKE VALOR AND KEEP OUT INTRUDERS.
NO LUCK ...?
NOPE. I GUESS THEY DON'T KNOW ANY-THING AFTER ALL.
AND YOU CAME OUT ALL THIS WAY FROM THE INTERNA-TIONAL POLICE HEADQUAR—
DON'T WORRY ABOUT IT.
I'LL LEAVE THIS POKÉ-MON HERE.
POINK
KEEP AN EYE ON THINGS FOR ME!
FWP
HM ... WHO'S THAT ...?

THE CONCERNED CITIZEN WHO CAPTURED THOSE TWO AND BROUGHT THEM IN FOR QUESTIONING.
AHHHHHH...
APPARENTLY THERE'S SOMETHING HE WANTS TO ASK THEM... SO HE'S BEEN WAITING UNTIL WE WERE DONE INTER-VIEWING THEM.
I CAN'T WAIT TO RECORD THE FOOTPRINTS OF THEIR KRICKETUNE AND DRAPION!
I WISH THEY'D HURRY UP AND FINISH!
OH...
WHERE AM I...?

THE SAME THING HAS BEEN HAPPENING TO EVERYONE THROUGHOUT THE SINNOH REGION.
HERE ONE SECOND... THERE THE NEXT...
BEBE
SNIPPETS OF TIME REPEATING OVER AND OVER...
PEOPLE THROWN INTO CHAOS, PARALYZED WITH FEAR...
...AS THE SPACE-TIME ANOMALY CONTINUES TO GROW AND THREATEN EVERYDAY EXISTENCE!

HA HA HA... SCARED?
TERRI-FIED?
YOU ARE ONLY EXPERI-ENCING FEAR...
...BE-CAUSE YOUR HEART IS INCOM-PLETE.
EMOTIONS SUCH AS FEAR CAN BE CON-TROLLED THROUGH WILL-POWER.
IF YOU HAVE THE KNOWL-EDGE TO INCREASE YOUR WILL-POWER...
EMOTION, WILL-POWER, KNOWL-EDGE...
WHEN THE THREE SUPPORT AND REGULATE EACH OTHER...
...PER-FECTION WILL BE ACHIEVED.
BUT LOOK AT THIS WORLD!!
ALWAYS LACKING AT LEAST ONE OF THE THREE, IT HAS SPIRALED OUT OF CONTROL ...
... DETERIO-RATING INTO A STATE OF INCOM-PLETENESS BEYOND THE POINT OF REPAIR!!

THERE IS NO OPTION NOW BUT TO START FROM SCRATCH!!
THE CREATION OF A NEW UNIVERSE WILL BRING ABOUT A PERFECT WORLD!!
UNI
TIME AND SPACE.
UNIVERSE
SPACE AND TIME.
BY COMBINING DIALGA'S POWER OVER TIME AND PALKIA'S POWER OVER SPACE...
...A CORE WILL BE CREATED...
...THAT WILL BECOME THE SEED OF A NEW UNIVERSE!

RMBL
RMBL
RMBL
RMBL
FLOAT
EVERY-THING INCOM-PLETE WILL BE ERADI-CATED!
HA HA HA HA HA!
AND THUS BEGINS A PERFECT NEW WORLD!!

YOU HAVE GOT TO BE KID-DING ME!!
GRAB
CRASHER WAKE !!
BOOING
YOU HAVE TO STOP THEM !!
BOM
PULL
WACK

FAN-TINA, WAKE UP...!!
DRG DRG DRG
YOU HAVE TO FIGHT IT!!
BOM
DRIF-BLIM, HELP ME!!
RSSSSHH
IT'S... NO USE ...
NO!!

HANG IN THERE, EVERY-BODY!!
I'M GOING TO CLOSE THAT HOLE!!
MOO!!
BLIZ-ZARD!!
HWITT

A POINTLESS EFFORT. DID YOU SERIOUSLY THINK ATTACKING IT WOULD DO ANY GOOD?
WELL THEN...
...I'LL JUMP INTO THE HOLE MYSELF!
C'MON, MOO! LET'S GO!!
KTH
UD
KTH
UD
LET'S SEE IF WE CAN CLOSE THIS HOLE FROM THE INSIDE!!
JUMP
RSSHH

DIA-A-A-A!!
NO-O-O-O-O!!
RTTL
RTTL
RTTL
ZIP
BOM
SHUNK
HUH?
WE... STOPPED?

UH... PLATINUM? WHAT'S GOING ON?
I... DON'T KNOW !!
BUT THAT POKÉMON CLEARLY JUMPED OUT OF YOUR BAG!
BUT ...
...THAT POKÉ BALL...
?!
IT WAS... THAT POKÉ BALL WAS INSIDE MY BAG...
TINK

WHY DID IT APPEAR ALL OF A SUD-DEN?!
JUST WHEN DIA TRIED TO ENTER THE RIFT?!
AND, UH... IS THIS POKÉMON ON **OUR** SIDE?!
OH YES! IT'S DEFI-NITELY ON YOUR SIDE.

THE FOOTPRINT SAYS... "I'VE BEEN WAITING TO RECEIVE MY ORDERS.
TUNK
I CAN CLEARLY DISCERN THAT FROM ITS FOOT-PRINT.
"I WILL...
"...FIGHT FOR SINNOH.
"I'LL GIVE IT MY ALL."
R-S-T-L
GOT IT!
YOU SEE ...?
DR. FOOT-STEP!!

ADVENTURE MAP
DIAMOND
Spear Pillar
TRU
Torterra ♂
KIT
Lickilicky ♂
LAX
Munchlax ♂
MOO
Mamoswine ♂
DON
Shieldon ♂
?
PEARL
Spear Pillar
CHIMLER
Infernape ♂
ZELLER
Buizel ♂
CHATLER
Chatot ♂
TAULER
Tauros ♂
RAYLER
Luxray ♂
DIGLER
Diglett ♂
PLATINUM
Spear Pillar
EMPOLEON
Empoleon ♀
LOPUNNY
Lopunny ♀
RAPIDASH
Rapidash ♂
Oreburgh
VS Roark
Coal Badge
Eterna
VS Gardenia
Forest Badge
Veilstone
VS Maylene
Cobble Badge
Pastoria
VS Wake
Fen Badge
Hearthome
VS Fantina
Relic Badge
Canalave
VS Byron
Mine Badge
Snowpoint City
VS Candice
Icicle Badge
Sunyshore City
VS Volker
Beacon Badge

79

Double Trouble with Dialga and Palkia VI

AT ANY RATE, DR. FOOTSTEP'S READINGS OF FOOTPRINTS ARE ACCURATE. THAT HUGE POKÉMON IS DEFINITELY ON OUR SIDE!
ON THE BRIGHT SIDE, IT LOOKS LIKE I'LL BE ABLE TO GATHER AN AMAZING FOOTPRINT AT THIS LOCATION!
UM... NOT IF THE FOOT **CRUSHES** YOU **FIRST**!
DR. FOOT-STEP!! WHAT ARE YOU DOING HERE?!
I DON'T RIGHTLY KNOW... I STEPPED OUT OF THE POLICE STATION...AND WOUND UP **HERE**!
REGI-GIGAS !!
ISN'T THAT RIGHT, LADY...?
YES!
DNK
DNK
DNK
DUN
DUN
DUN
KERR
SMASH

IT CAPTURED BOTH OF THEM!! TWO LEGENDARY POKÉMON AT ONCE!!
IF WE CAN STOP DIALGA AND PALKIA FROM FIGHTING AND CLOSE THAT HOLE...
THAT "CORE" THINGIE WILL QUIT SPREAD-ING!!

WOW! AMAZ-ING!!
SMAK
KATHUNK
DIA!!
OW...
WHY MUST YOU ALWAYS GET IN MY WAY?
DON'T YOU UNDER-STAND...
...THE IMPOR-TANCE OF PERFEC-TION? OF MAKING THIS WORLD COM-PLETE?
DON'T YOU COMPRE-HEND...
...WHAT A GRAND THING IT IS THAT I HOPE TO ACHIEVE?

NO. IT'S BEYOND THE LIKES OF YOU.
YOU'VE NEVER EVEN CONSIDERED THE IMPLICATIONS OF TIME AND SPACE BEFORE!!
UH ...
I...DO UNDER-STAND.
I'M SLOW.
COM-PARED TO ME, PEARL IS FAST.
I... CAN'T USE BIG WORDS TO DESCRIBE IT, BUT...
EVEN WHEN WE DO THE SAME THING, PEARL DOES THEM QUICKLY AND I TAKE MY TIME.
EVEN THE SAME HOUR CAN FEEL LONG TO PEARL AND SHORT TO ME.
11:18
...I GET IT.

BUT... IT'S STILL THE SAME HOUR.
THAT'S HOW I'VE EXPERIENCED "TIME."
AND I'VE BEEN TRAVELING WITH PEARL AND LADY...
WE'D ONLY HEARD ABOUT PLACES AND TOWNS IN THIS AREA...
...SO THE PLACES WE WENT TO, THE PEOPLE WE MET, THE POKÉMON WE SAW—THEY WERE ALL NEW TO US. THAT'S HOW I DISCOVERED HOW BIG THIS WORLD IS.
THAT'S ...
...HOW I'VE EXPERIENCED "SPACE."

APPAR-ENTLY ASKING YOU WAS A COMPLETE WASTE OF BREATH...
YOU AND YOUR SILLY NOTIONS... AND YOU HAVE THE NERVE TO STAND IN MY WAY!
AS I THOUGHT...
...I MUST WIPE CLEAN THIS IMPERFECT WORLD!
WHY?
WHY...
...DO YOU GET TO DECIDE THAT?
THE TIME I SPENT WITH PEARL AND LADY...
...THE SPACE I TRAVELED THROUGH WITH THEM...
THAT TIME AND SPACE IS MORE IMPORTANT TO ME THAN ANYTHING!
THAT DOESN'T GO JUST FOR ME EITHER.
THERE ARE OTHER PEOPLE AND POKÉMON WHO CHERISH THIS WORLD, THIS TIME AND SPACE...
...AND THAT'S WHY THEY'RE ALL GATH-ERED HERE TODAY.

YOU HAVE NO RIGHT...
...TO TAKE AWAY THE THINGS THAT ARE PRECIOUS TO OTHERS FOR YOUR OWN SELFISH REASONS!!
WHAT ...?!
HOW ...?!

DIALGA!!
PALKIA!!
WHY HAVE THEY STOPPED FIGHTING?!
THEY'RE STILL UNDER MY CONTROL ...
AND THAT HUGE POKÉMON ISN'T STOPPING THEM...
IMPOS-SIBLE !!
COULD IT BE...? DID THEY STOP BATTLING... BECAUSE THEY'RE **LISTENING** TO **HIM**?!
HAVE THOSE LEGENDARY POKÉMON... SO IMMENSELY POWERFUL...BEEN TAKEN IN BY... THIS BOY?!

AAAAARGH !!
JINGL JINGL
DIALGA!!
PALKIA!!
DON'T STOP FIGHTING!!
I COMMAND YOU TO RESUME YOUR BATTLE !!

KRASH
LOOK !!
THE RED CHAIN !!
BECAUSE OF YOU, AZELF, UXIE AND MESPRIT ESCAPED BEFORE WE COULD CREATE THE SECOND RED CHAIN!
FORCING ME TO CREATE THIS CHAIN ARTIFI-CIALLY!!
BUT IT WAS INCOMPLETE! THE GYM LEADERS MANAGED TO TEAR IT APART!!
DIA !!
DIA-MOND !!
SMAKK
ALL BECAUSE IT WAS IMPER-FECT!!
OWW ...

I CAN'T BELIEVE YOU.
YOU'VE CER-TAINLY GOT GUTS.
HEAR-ING WHAT YOU SAID...
...MAKES ME VERY HAPPY.
I'M SO GLAD I GOT TO...
...TRAVEL WITH YOU TOO!
BUT...

...IT SEEMS LIKE I'VE...
...MADE THE BATTLE BETWEEN DIALGA AND PALKIA...
...EVEN WORSE!
AND THAT OTHER POKÉMON—IT'S BEEN INJURED.
OH... LADY!
HAVE YOU DECIPHERED THE SCROLL YET?!
YES! I MANAGED TO READ IT ALL!!
ACCORDING TO THE TEXT...
...THESE TWO ARE **PERFECT COUNTERPARTS**!

TIME AND SPACE ...
THE LUSTROUS ORB AND THE ADAMANT ORB...
THE ROAR OF TIME, DIALGA'S GREATEST MOVE, WHICH HAS THE POWER TO BLAST AWAY TIME, AND...
...SPACIAL REND, PALKIA'S GREATEST MOVE, WHICH HAS THE POWER TO TEAR AWAY SPACE...
THEY'RE BOTH EQUALLY BALANCED AGAINST EACH OTHER.
SO ...
THERE ARE TWO OF THEM ...
... BUT ...
...ONLY ONE RED CHAIN...
CYRUS CAN'T CON-TROL BOTH OF THEM WITH A SINGLE CHAIN.
SOONER OR LATER, THE MOMENT WILL COME WHEN THE CLASH BETWEEN THESE TWO POWERS BECOMES IMBAL-ANCED.
AND THAT'S OUR OPPORTU-NITY...
NOD

WE HAVE TO ATTACK WITH...
...EVERYTHING WE'VE GOT!!
DROP
THUD
SMASH

WHAT ?!
ARRRGH!!
PALKIA-A-A-A!!
NOW !!
THUMP
TH UNK
SMASH

TING

DEEP AND QUIET EMOTIONS.
STRONG IRON-CLAD WILLPOWER.
AND...
...WHEN YOU ADD TO THAT KNOWLEDGE...

I SEE...
EVEN THOUGH THEY ARE INCOMPLETE...
THEY JOINED HANDS AND SUPPORTED EACH OTHER. THAT'S WHY...
...THEY WERE ABLE TO STOP ME.
THAT'S WHY...

THE HOLE IS FADING AWAY!
AND THE DISTORTION IS GONE TOO!
HEY...
WHAT ABOUT CYRUS?
HE'S ALIVE...
...BUT INJURED—PHYSICALLY AND MENTALLY.

THAT MEANS TEAM GALAC-TIC'S PLOT IS FINISHED TOO!
THEIR EVIL ORGANI-ZATION IS BOUND TO FALL APART NOW...
AND BEST OF ALL...
...DIALGA AND PALKIA HAVE CALMED DOWN!
I GUESS WE CAN'T EXACTLY CALL THIS A HAPPY ENDING, BUT...
...WE HAVE...
...SAVED THE WORLD!
BMP

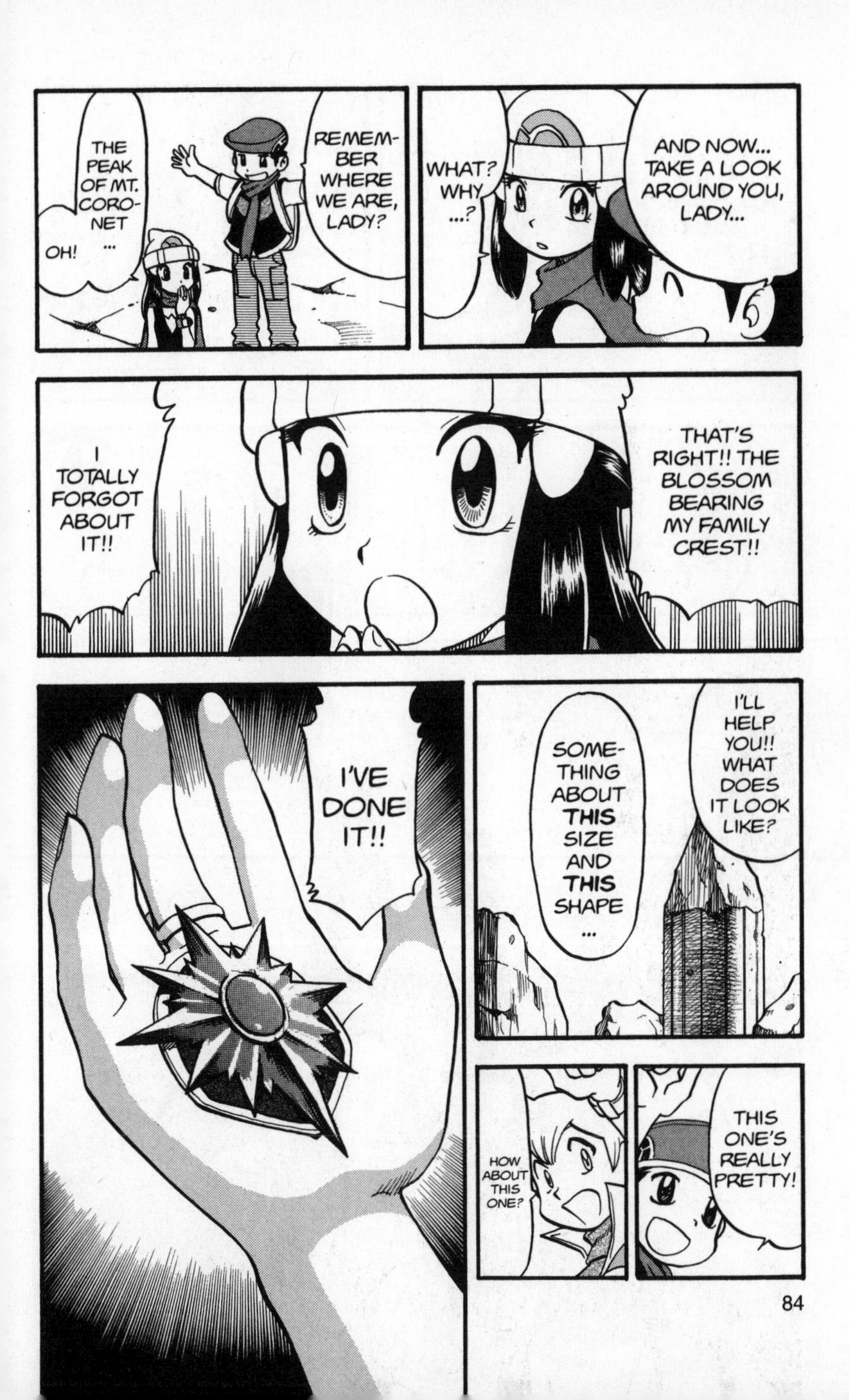
REMEMBER WHERE WE ARE, LADY?
THE PEAK OF MT. CORONET ...
OH!
AND NOW... TAKE A LOOK AROUND YOU, LADY...
WHAT? WHY ...?
THAT'S RIGHT!! THE BLOSSOM BEARING MY FAMILY CREST!!
I TOTALLY FORGOT ABOUT IT!!
I'LL HELP YOU!! WHAT DOES IT LOOK LIKE?
SOMETHING ABOUT THIS SIZE AND THIS SHAPE ...
THIS ONE'S REALLY PRETTY!
HOW ABOUT THIS ONE?
I'VE DONE IT!!

YOU'VE ACCOMPLISHED WHAT YOU SET OUT TO DO!
YES!
BUT THERE'S STILL ONE THING LEFT UNFINISHED...
EVEN THOUGH THEY'RE FAR FROM HERE...
IF I CAN JUST FIND THEM... I MIGHT BE ABLE TO HELP THEM TOO!
YOU'RE TALKING ABOUT PAKA AND UJI, AREN'T YOU?!
YES.
HEY!
EVEN THOUGH I'VE NEVER EVEN MET THEM...
LIKE YOU TWO, THEY GAVE THEIR ALL TO PROTECT ME...
I WANT TO FIND THEM!
I **HAVE** TO FIND THEM!! NO MATTER WHAT IT TAKES!

PAKA AND UJI GOT SUCKED INTO SOME KIND OF WEIRD VOID CREATED BY TEAM GALACTIC'S MACHINE...
THE QUICKEST WAY TO FIND THEM WOULD BE TO ASK TEAM GALACTIC WHERE THEY WENT...
BUT IT DOESN'T LOOK LIKE WE'LL BE ABLE TO ASK CYRUS **ANYTHING** FOR A WHILE YET...
FOR NOW, WE'D BETTER TAKE HIM TO A HOSPITAL WITH THE OTHER INJURED GYM LEADERS.
THUNK
THUNK

REGI-GIGAS...
ANOTHER ONE OF SINNOH'S LEGEND-ARY POKÉMON.
I WANT IT, I WANT IT!

I HAVE TO MEASURE THE NUMBER OF UNITS BEFORE IT DISAPPEARS.
I MUSTN'T FORGET WHAT I CAME HERE FOR!
NO ...
IF ONLY I WERE A LITTLE CLOSER ...
SHOULD I STILL GIVE IT A TRY?
NO, NO, NO!
I'M SO GLAD THEY'RE ALL MISTAKEN ABOUT THAT THING...
DO THEY SERIOUSLY BELIEVE THAT'S A SEED THAT WILL TURN INTO A NEW UNIVERSE?
WHAT SIMPLETONS.
WHAT DID YOU SAY? DATA FOR WHAT ...?
SMASH
SHINE!
PEARL! THERE'S SOMEBODY OVER THERE!
WHAT ?!
OOPS! SHOOT... I WON'T BE ABLE TO GATHER THAT DATA AFTER ALL... I'VE GOT TO MAKE A RUN FOR IT!

AS A SCIENTIST, THAT'S A STATEMENT I CAN'T OVERLOOK!
PROFES-SOR ROWAN !!
BYRON !!
FATHER !!
HOW DID YOU GET HERE FROM UNDER-GROUND ...?
YOU'RE NOT GOING ANY-WHERE !!
CATCH
HAND OVER THAT DEVICE— NOW!
AGH! STOP IT!

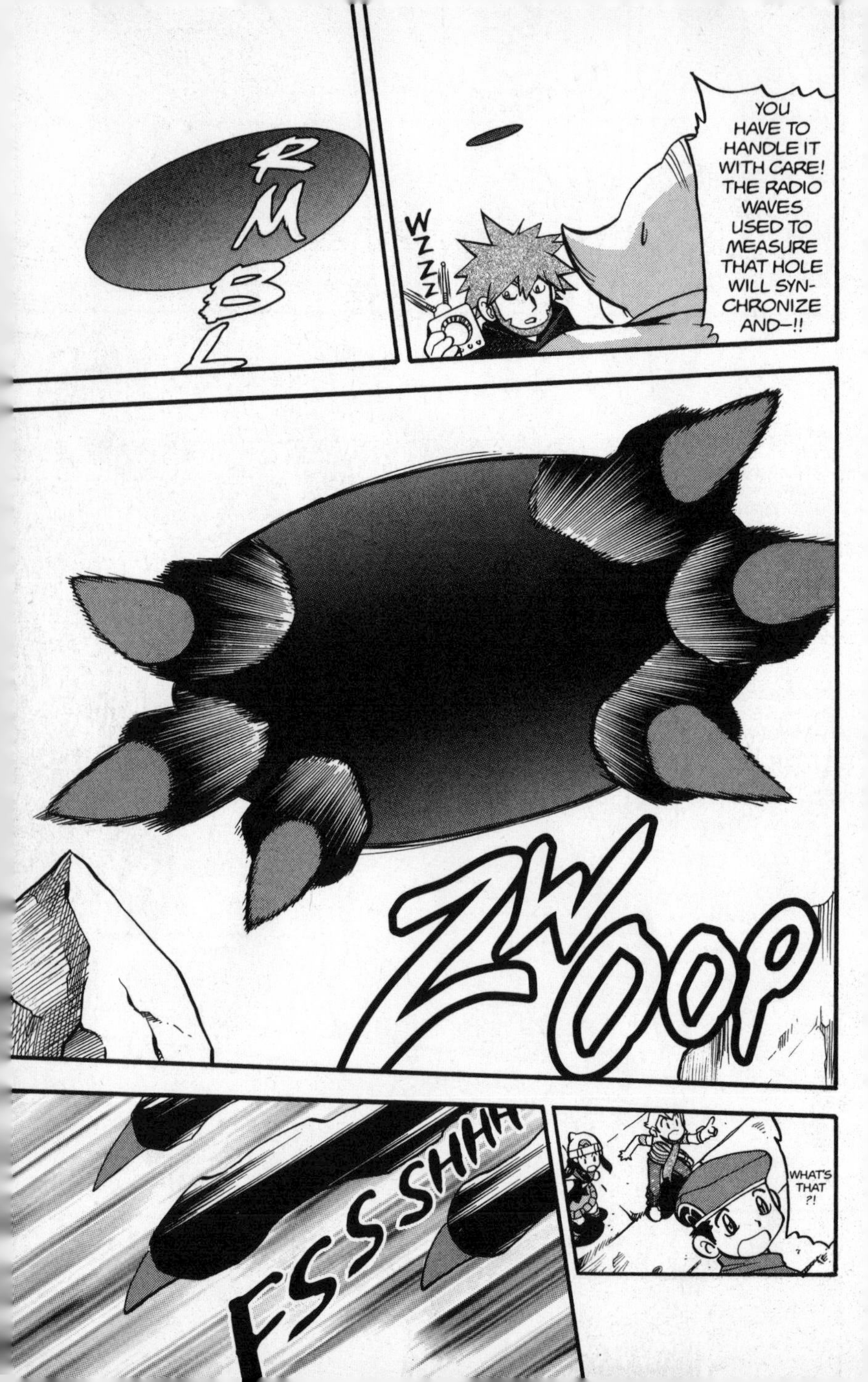
RMBL
WZZZ
YOU HAVE TO HANDLE IT WITH CARE! THE RADIO WAVES USED TO MEASURE THAT HOLE WILL SYN-CHRONIZE AND—!!
ZWOOP
FSSSHHH
WHAT'S THAT ?!

GRAB
GRAB
GRAB
FFF
FF
PP
PP
FF
DIALGA! PALKIA!
CYRUS TOO!!
THEY GOT SUCKED INSIDE!
PF

TING
SLITHR SLITHR

SEE? WHAT DID I TELL YOU? HEE HEE HEE!!
WAS THAT A POKÉMON INSIDE THAT HOLE?! ANSWER ME!!
YOUNG LADY...
DO YOU KNOW...
...ABOUT THE OTHER SIDE OF THE WORLD?
IF YOU DON'T...
...THEN YOU'D BETTER LEARN FAST.
MY NAME IS CHARON.
REMEMBER THAT!

BAMMF
GOOD-BYE!!
KOF KOF!!
WHERE DID HE GO?!
BOOOING
WHOA!!
SMUK
FWWIPP
TOO BAD... YOU JUST MISSED HIM.
I WONDER WHAT IT IS...?
BLEH
WHAT? YOU GOT THAT FROM HIM?

FLINT?
IT'S ME, VOLKNER.
I'M AT THE SPRING PATH THAT LEADS TO THE SENDOFF SPRING.
THERE'S AN EERIE LOOKING HOLE IN THE SKY IN FRONT OF ME.
AHA HA HA!! AND...?
HOW DOES IT MAKE YOU FEEL?
EXCITED?
YEAH! REALLY EXCITED.
AND WHY IS THAT?
HM...
ISN'T IT OBVIOUS?
IT'S BECAUSE I SENSE THE PRESENCE OF A POWERFUL BEING INSIDE IT!

WONDERFUL. LET'S INVESTIGATE THAT HOLE TOGETHER.
CAN YOU JOIN ME?
SURE.
HURRY UP THOUGH.
WHERE ARE YOU?
ME? I'M AT...
...THE BATTLE ZONE!
EVERYBODY IS HEADING BACK...
...TO WHERE THEY BELONG...

TWO WEEKS LATER ...
WE'RE SETTING SAIL... FINALLY!
HOW MANY YEARS HAS IT BEEN, PROFES-SOR?
TOO LONG FOR ME TO RE-CALL.
AND YOU'RE WEARING YOUR EMBLEM TOO.
IS IT BECAUSE YOU'RE GOING TO SEE YOUR FAMILY AGAIN AFTER SUCH A LONG TIME?
THAT TOO, BUT... HOW CAN I EXPLAIN...? IT'S A TRADITION... IT'S CEREMONIAL...
I MADE MY CREST FROM VEGETATION I FOUND ON THE TOP OF MT. CORONET WHEN I WAS YOUNG.
IT'S A FAMILY TRADITION THAT HAS BEEN PASSED DOWN FOR GENERA-TIONS.
TO YOUR DAUGH-TER AS WELL?
YES. SHE HAS ONE TOO. SHE'S TWELVE, SO IT WAS A LITTLE EARLY FOR HER...BUT SHE WENT ON HER QUEST TO THE MOUNTAIN AS WELL.
I NEVER DREAMED SHE'D GET CAUGHT UP IN SUCH CATACLYSMIC EVENTS ON HER JOURNEY!

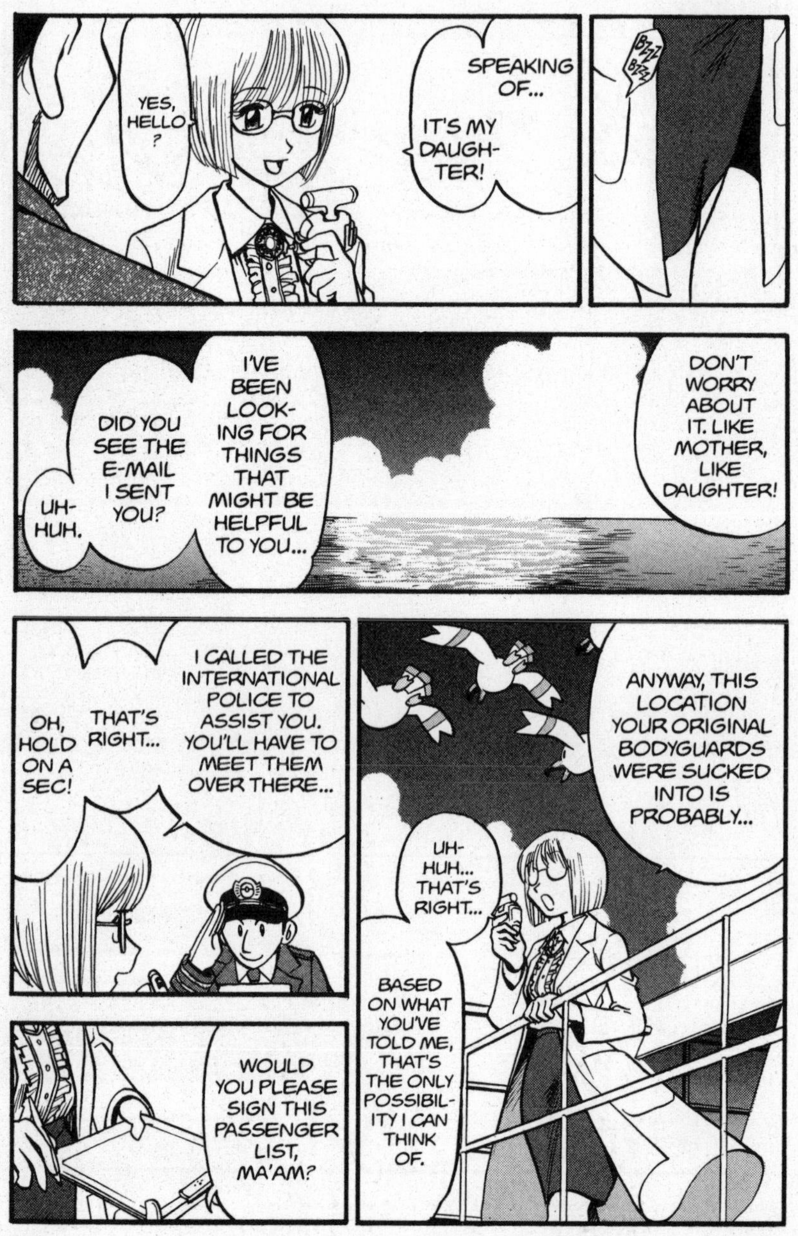
BZZZ BZZZ
SPEAKING OF...
IT'S MY DAUGHTER!
YES, HELLO?
DON'T WORRY ABOUT IT. LIKE MOTHER, LIKE DAUGHTER!
I'VE BEEN LOOKING FOR THINGS THAT MIGHT BE HELPFUL TO YOU...
DID YOU SEE THE E-MAIL I SENT YOU?
UH-HUH.
ANYWAY, THIS LOCATION YOUR ORIGINAL BODYGUARDS WERE SUCKED INTO IS PROBABLY...
UH-HUH... THAT'S RIGHT...
BASED ON WHAT YOU'VE TOLD ME, THAT'S THE ONLY POSSIBILITY I CAN THINK OF.
I CALLED THE INTERNATIONAL POLICE TO ASSIST YOU. YOU'LL HAVE TO MEET THEM OVER THERE...
THAT'S RIGHT...
OH, HOLD ON A SEC!
WOULD YOU PLEASE SIGN THIS PASSENGER LIST, MA'AM?

Yanase Berlitz

GOT THAT ...?
INVESTIGATE THE DISTORTION WORLD.
GO TO THE DISTORTION WORLD...
... PLATINUM !!
POKéMON ADVENTURES™
DIAMOND * PEARL
Fin

THE BATTLE ZONE...
LOCATED OUTSIDE THE SINNOH REGION, THE BATTLE ZONE CONSISTS OF...
THE FIGHT AREA.
THE SURVIVAL AREA.
AND THE RESORT AREA.
NOW WITHIN THESE THREE AREAS...
...A NEW STORY IS ABOUT TO UNFOLD.
IT ALL BEGINS IN A BEAUTIFUL RESORT VILLA...

My dear friends Diamond and Pearl have set out on a journey...
Thank you very much for all the advice. I'm writing to update you on my recent activities.
Dear Mother,
...to investigate several legendary Pokémon they read about....
...in the journal of a mysterious man named Charon...
...who appears to have been working for Team Galactic before his disappearance.
There's something I have to take care of as well.
Today, I set foot in an area called the Battle Zone for the very first time.
I'm alone and I feel lonely. But I must face my fears.
Wish me well on my journey. At the moment, I'm hoping my meeting with an officer of the International Police goes smoothly.
I'll write again soon,
Your devoted daughter, Platinum

The Eighth Chapter

PLATINUM

Adventure 80
Leaping Past Lopunny

ARE YOU SURE ABOUT THIS?
DO YOU REALLY WANT TO LET GO OF SUCH A BEAUTIFUL VILLA?
YES, IT'S FINE.
GO AHEAD AND DO THE HONORS.
Seven Stone
SKRTCH SKRTCH
ALL RIGHT THEN. I'LL TAKE CARE OF THE REST.
I HEARD YOU CAME TO THE SINNOH REGION IN SEARCH OF RARE STONES.
YES. AND I BUILT THIS VILLA AS MY BASE OF OPERA-TIONS.
BUT I'VE GATH-ERED ALL THE STONES I CAME FOR.
THEY DON'T NEED A STONE COLLECTOR IN THIS REGION ANYMORE.
HELLO...? FATHER ...?
YES, I'M DEPARTING FOR THE HOENN REGION IN JUST A MOMENT...

THANKS FOR TAKING CARE OF THE REST OF THE PAPERWORK.
BOOM
SAFE TRAVELS!!
WOW... RICH PEOPLE! HA!
THEY CUSTOM BUILD A HUGE VILLA LIKE THIS AND THEN SELL IT OFF LIKE IT'S NOTHING TO THEM.
OH WELL.
LET'S SEE WHO THE NEW OWNER IS...
WHOA! THIS ONE'S WEALTHY TOO!!
SUPER SUPER **SUPER** WEALTHY!!
MEANWHILE, IN THE SURVIVAL AREA...
BATTLEGROUND
Members Only
THE BATTLEGROUND...
ALL RIGHT! LET'S HAVE OURSELVES A BATTLE!!
ALAKAZAM, **PSYCHIC**!!
MY POKÉMON IS FULL OF LIFE, YOU KNOW.
BLISSEY, **HYPER BEAM**.
YEAH! LET'S POKÉMON BATTLE!! HA HA HA...
CLAYDOL, **CALM MIND**!!
NO WAY AM I GONNA LOSE...
ARCANINE, **FLARE BLITZ**.

THUMP
DUNK
S'MAK
SH
A
R
K
THE BATTLE-GROUND.
THIS IS WHERE SKILLED POKÉMON TRAINERS GO TO TAKE PART IN **ADVANCED** POKÉMON BATTLES.
BATTLEGROUND
Members Only
LOOK AT THEM GO!
HM ...

MAYBE...
...I'LL MEET TRAINERS WITH VALUABLE INFORMATION HERE.
SHLURP
TIME TO START MY INVESTI-GATION!!
INTERNATIONAL POLICE EQUIPMENT NO. 1!!!
EXCELLENT SCOPE!!
PLUNK
SET UP!!
ZOOM UP!!
SQUEEKSQUEEK
SQUEEK
KRIK
OOPS!

HM... PERHAPS SHOPPING IN THE DISCOUNT SECTION WASN'T SUCH A GOOD IDEA AFTER ALL...
SEEMS LIKE THIS ALWAYS HAPPENS WHENEVER I TRY TO SAVE A FEW BUCKS...
GUESS I HAVE NO CHOICE BUT TO... INFILTRATE!!
INTERNATIONAL POLICE EQUIPMENT NO. 2! INVISIBLE CLOTH!!
SHFL SHFL
HA HA HA... I'VE MANAGED TO INFILTRATE THE BATTLEGROUND—WHICH IS ONLY OPEN TO MEMBERS.
SLIPPED RIGHT BY EVERYONE!
..
HOLD ON A MINUTE!!
HMPH...
FWIP FWIP
AH!!
WHO'S HIDING UNDER THERE?!
RUSH
HEY, YOU! YOU LOOK SUSPICIOUS!
MY BIG BROTHER IS ONE OF THE ELITE FOUR, YOU KNOW!! DON'T MAKE ME GO AND CALL HIM!

FSSH
AH!
HE NOTICED THAT I WAS OUT OF THE ORDINARY! HOW PERCEPTIVE!!
FWIP FWIP FWIP
HEY!
I WAS HOPING TO GATHER SOME INFORMATION HERE BEFORE ATTENDING MY MEETING...
BUT IT LOOKS LIKE IT MIGHT BE SHREWDER FOR ME TO HEAD THERE POST HASTE!
WHAT A WON-DERFUL VILLA!
THIS WILL BE THE PERFECT PLACE FOR A HOME BASE RIGHT BY THE BATTLE ZONE.

PLEASE SIGN THIS... AND THIS...
OF COURSE.
platinum
AND THAT COMPLETES OUR TRANSACTION!
EXCUSE ME...
IS THAT THE PERSON I'M SUPPOSED TO MEET?
I WAS TOLD MY CONTACT WOULD MOVE INTO THIS VILLA TODAY...
DOES THAT MEAN ...?!
...THIS GIRL IS MY CONTACT ?!
LUCKILY WE AGREED UPON A CODE TO IDENTIFY EACH OTHER.
BUT BEFORE I TRY THAT...
...I'LL CHECK OUT HER BATTLE SKILLS!
TOSS
EQUIPMENT NO. 3! VARIABLE ROPE!!

KLATTER
ZOOP
TING
LOPUNNY!!
FOCUS BLAST!!
KATHUNK

ODD.
VERY ODD.
I THOUGHT FOR SURE I SENSED SOMEBODY'S PRESENCE...
A... ROCK?
HM.
SPLENDID!
KE-RAK
WHAT?
HUH?
EQUIPMENT NO. 4! PROTECTION ROCK!
YOU'RE AS SKILLED AS THEY SAY.
"FAITH CAN ...
AH!!
"...MOVE MOUNTAINS."

THE SECRET...
...CODE!
SO YOU'RE THE PERSON I'M SUPPOSED TO MEET?
MY CONTACT FROM THE INTERNA-TIONAL POLICE?
PRE-CISELY.
THE **REAL** PER-SON?
AS REAL AS EVER!
OR...ARE YOU JUST ABOUT TO GO ON A TOUR OF SANDGEM PARK OR SOMETHING?
NO.
OR... MAYBE IN REALITY YOU'RE A COMEDIAN?
NO.
I DID IT! THIS MEETING IS A SUCCESS! I MANAGED TO MEET THE PERSON I WAS SUPPOSED TO!!
A HUGE SUCCESS, RIGHT, RAPIDASH, EMPOLEON, LOPUNNY?
YES.

NOT TO WORRY! I AM AN INTERNATIONAL POLICE OFFICER. THE GENUINE ARTICLE.
AT TIMES, I'LL BE ON TOP OF AN AERIAL TRAMWAY.
AT TIMES, I'LL BE BEHIND A TOWER.
AT TIMES, I'LL BE ON A SHIP.
...MY COMRADES ARE ALL OVER THE GLOBE...
WE LITERALLY TRAVEL ALL AROUND THE WORLD TO DO OUR JOB!!
AT THIS VERY MOMENT ...
... SEARCHING FOR EVIL-DOERS!!

SO... WHAT'S YOUR NAME?
"LOOKER."
YOUR GIVEN NAME? YOUR CODE NAME?
SOME-THING TO CALL YOU BY...?
THAT'S WHAT EVERYBODY CALLS ME.
VERY WELL.
AND I AM PLATINUM BERLITZ.
I'M A DEDI-CATED POKÉ-MON TRAINER OF THE SINNOH REGION.
PROFESSOR ROWAN AND MY FATHER WERE MY TEACHERS.

LOOKS LIKE WE'RE GOING TO BE PARTNERS!
NICE TO MEET YOU.
IT'S A PLEASURE TO MEET YOU.
ALL MANNER OF SKILLED POKÉMON TRAINERS GATHER HERE AT THE BATTLE FRONTIER INSIDE THE BATTLE ZONE.
NOT TO MEN-TION...
FAMOUS TRAINERS TOO. I'M POSITIVE THAT **SOME-WHERE** AMONGST THEM...
...IS **SOMEONE** WITH INFORMATION ABOUT THE EVILDOERS I'M PURSUING.
...SOME-ONE WITH INFORMA-TION...
...ABOUT THE DIS-TORTION WORLD...
...THAT **YOU** ARE SEEKING!!

BATTLE FRONTIER RULE BOOK

THE BATTLE FRONTIER HAS FIVE DIFFERENT FACILITIES WHERE YOU CAN TAKE PART IN A VARIETY OF POKÉMON BATTLES. OF COURSE, THESE BATTLES ARE GOVERNED BY STRICT RULES (BELOW), SO WE REQUEST THAT CHALLENGERS READ THROUGH THEM CAREFULLY.

Basic Rule ①

Limits on Pokémon Usage

WE HAVE ESTABLISHED A LIMIT AS TO WHAT KIND OF POKÉMON YOU MAY USE WHEN PARTICIPATING IN A BATTLE AT EACH OF THE FACILITIES. THE USE OF LEGENDARY POKÉMON MUST BE PRE-APPROVED. POKÉMON EGGS MAY NOT PARTICIPATE.

Basic Rule ②

Bringing Items and Use of Items

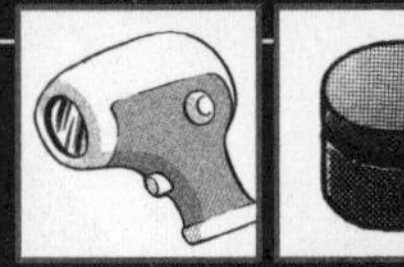

YOU ARE ALLOWED TO BRING ITEMS INTO BATTLE HALL. YOU MAY ALSO BRING ITEMS INTO BATTLE TOWER, BUT YOU ARE NOT ALLOWED TO BRING MORE THAN ONE POKÉMON WITH THE SAME ITEM. IN BATTLE FACTORY, BATTLE ARCADE AND BATTLE CASTLE, YOU ARE NOT ALLOWED TO BRING IN YOUR OWN ITEMS. HOWEVER, IN BATTLE FACTORY, YOU MAY USE AN ITEM IF THE RENTAL POKÉMON IS HOLDING ONE. FOR BATTLE ARCADE, YOU MAY USE AN ITEM IF THE ROULETTE MACHINE LANDS ON AN ITEM BOX. FOR BATTLE CASTLE, YOU MAY USE AN ITEM ONCE YOU BUY AN ITEM USING CASTLE POINTS.

Basic Rule ③

Allowable Moves

EACH POKÉMON WILL ONLY BE ALLOWED TO USE FOUR MOVES. THEY ARE NOT ALLOWED TO USE ANY OTHER MOVE APART FROM THE FOUR WHICH YOU HAVE REGISTERED IN ADVANCE

Adventure 81
Deprogramming Porygon-Z
POKÉMON ADVENTURES

GOOD MORNING, EVERYBODY.
AS ALWAYS, I'M SURE WE'LL HAVE MANY POKÉMON TRAINERS HERE TODAY TO CHALLENGE YOU. SO PULL UP YOUR SOCKS AND PREPARE TO FACE THEM!
AFTER ALL, WE ARE...
...THE FRONTIER BRAIN!
THAT'S IT FOR THIS MORNING'S MEETING.
YOU MAY HEAD BACK TO YOUR FACILITIES NOW.
DAHLIA, TO BATTLE ARCADE!
THOR-TON...
...TO BATTLE FAC-TORY!
AND ARGENTA, HEAD OVER TO BATTLE HALL!

CHUK
SWSH
SWSH
SWSH
BONEMERANG!
SO, YOU'RE HERE ...!
SWSH
RILEY!
SNAG
IT'S BEEN A MONTH SINCE THIS PLACE OPENED.
AND IT LOOKS LIKE IT'S GOING TO BE A HUGE SUC-CESS.
THIS BATTLE FRONTIER IS AS GOOD AS THE ONES I'VE SEEN IN OTHER REGIONS.
THANKS.
FROM WHAT I HEAR, YOU'VE HAD A PRETTY ROUGH TIME LATELY ...

YOU WERE THERE, WEREN'T YOU? AT THE SCENE OF...THE INCIDENT...
HEY!
STOP!!
KLATR
BUT...THE PERSON I FOUGHT...
...DISAP-PEARED.
AND THREE OTHERS...
WELL, I'M CONVINCED THEY WENT SOMEWHERE TO REGROUP.

I CAN HARDLY SENSE AN AURA FROM THIS MACHINE ANYMORE.
IN OTHER WORDS... I'VE RUN OUT OF LEADS.
I SEE ...
I WAS WONDERING IF THERE WAS A WAY TO FIX THIS MACHINE SO IT COULD FLY AGAIN...
HM ...
I KNOW OF A GUY WHO COULD DO IT!
YOU DO?!
SOMEONE WHO'S REALLY GOOD AT INVENTING AND FIXING GADGETS.
HOLD ON A SEC.
MR. PALMER, THE GATE'S READY!
GREAT !!

RMBL RMBL
OOOH...
OPEN THE GATE!!
MUMBL
MUMBLE

WHICH CHAL- LENGE ARE YOU GOING TO TAKE ON TODAY?!
HM... I DID PRETTY WELL AT THE FACTORY YESTERDAY, SO...
LET'S GO TO THE TOWER— THE BATTLE TOWER !!
OH NO! I'LL NEVER BE ABLE TO WIN THERE!
HELLO.
IS THIS YOUR FIRST TIME AT THE BATTLE FRON- TIER?
I WILL BE YOUR GUIDE.
WHICH FACILITY ARE YOU CONSID- ERING?
FACTORY? ARCADE? CASTLE? HALL? TOWER?
THANK YOU...
BUT I'M FINE. I'VE STUDIED ALL THE RULES IN ADVANCE.
I CAN EXPLAIN THE RULES OF EACH LOCATION TO YOU IF YOU WISH.
HM!
ALL OF THEM ?!
YES.
THERE ARE FIVE FACILITIES AT THE BATTLE FRONTIER. THE TRAINER'S GOAL IS TO OVERCOME THE CHALLENGES AT EACH FACILITY.

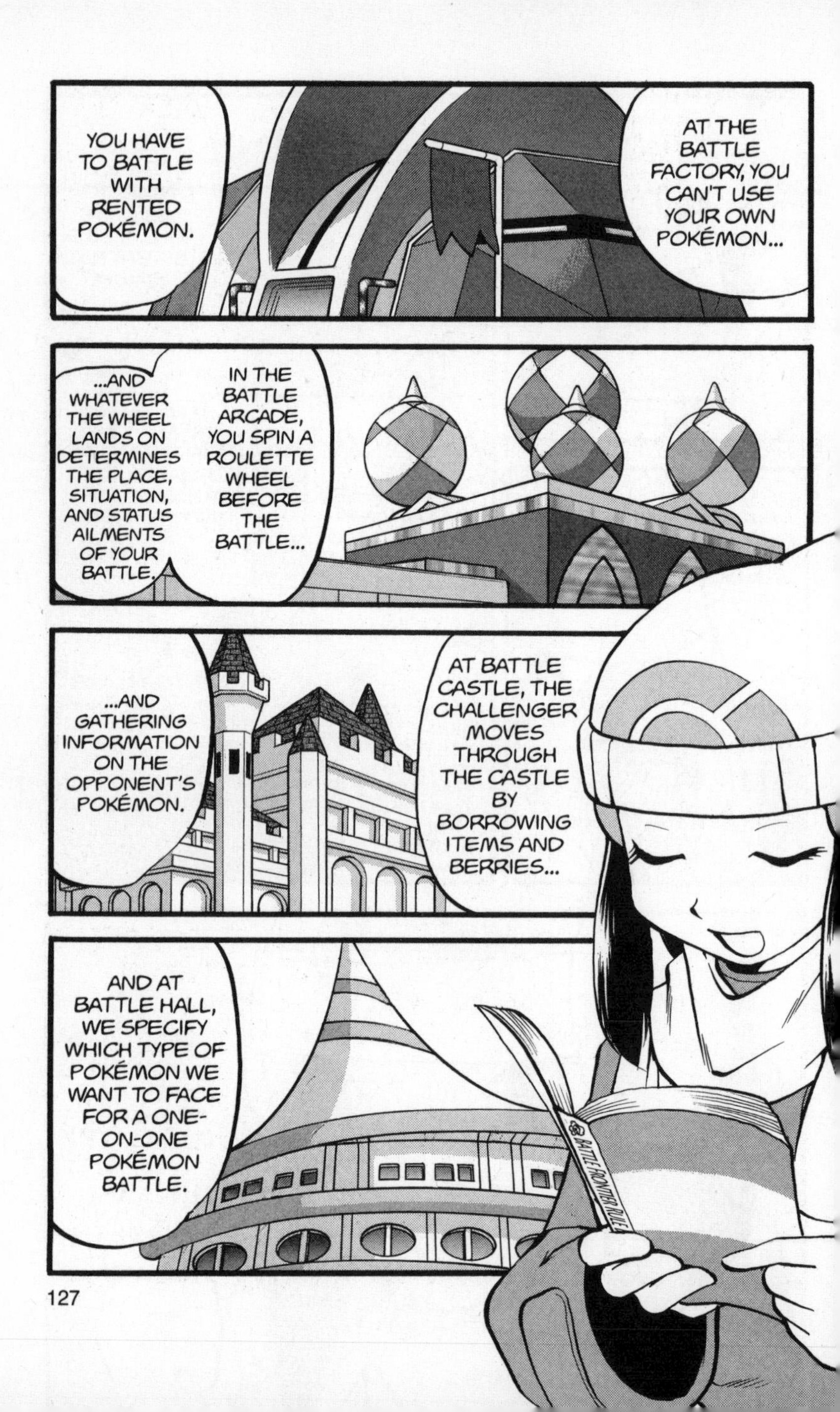
AT THE BATTLE FACTORY, YOU CAN'T USE YOUR OWN POKÉMON...
YOU HAVE TO BATTLE WITH RENTED POKÉMON.
IN THE BATTLE ARCADE, YOU SPIN A ROULETTE WHEEL BEFORE THE BATTLE...
...AND WHATEVER THE WHEEL LANDS ON DETERMINES THE PLACE, SITUATION, AND STATUS AILMENTS OF YOUR BATTLE.
AT BATTLE CASTLE, THE CHALLENGER MOVES THROUGH THE CASTLE BY BORROWING ITEMS AND BERRIES...
...AND GATHERING INFORMATION ON THE OPPONENT'S POKÉMON.
AND AT BATTLE HALL, WE SPECIFY WHICH TYPE OF POKÉMON WE WANT TO FACE FOR A ONE-ON-ONE POKÉMON BATTLE.
BATTLE FRONTIER RULE

I DON'T THINK I NEED TO EXPLAIN THE RULES OF BATTLE TOWER.
IT'S JUST A STRAIGHT-FORWARD POKÉMON BATTLE.
THE CHALLENGERS CONTINUE BATTLING TO MOVE UP THE LADDER.
THIS IS THE MOST FAMOUS OF THE BATTLE FACILITIES—AND THERE'S ONE JUST LIKE IT IN JOHTO AND HOENN AS WELL.
HM!
I WAS BRIEFED THAT YOU WERE A FINE LADY FROM A SCHOLARLY FAMILY, BUT...YOUR KNOWLEDGE IS TRULY AMAZING!
I'M IMPRES-SED!
WE DON'T NEED YOUR ASSISTANCE! NOW GO, GO!
BUT KNOWL-EDGE IS ONLY SUPERFI-CIAL.
Shoo! Shoo!
YOU CAN'T ACQUIRE TRUE UNDERSTANDING WITHOUT PERSONAL EXPERIENCE.
THAT'S WHY I MUST BATTLE...
...IN ALL THESE VENUES!

ATTA-GIRL!!
YOU'RE SENSIBLE—AND REFINED. A TRUE LADY!!
OH, NOW YOU'RE JUST FLATTERING ME...
NOT ME, MY LADY!!
YES?
YOU ADDRESSED ME?
HUH?

NO ...
I WAS SPEAKING TO LADY PLATINUM OVER THERE, NOT YOU.
SWISH
WHOA!! I GUESS THIS IS WHAT YOU'D CALL A "BOLT OUT OF THE BLUE"!
WHAT'S GOING ON ...?!
WOOSH

SWISH
WHAT THE ...?
HEY!
SNIKR
CUT IT OUT!
SNAK
BUT HIS ATTACK DIDN'T EVEN HIT ME!!
IT'S PSYCHO CUT!!
WHAT GIVES ?!
DRUP
DRUP
DRUP
MATERIALIZED BLADES CREATED BY GALLADE'S MIND CAME FLYING AT YOU!
LOOKS LIKE GAL-LADE ...

...IS TRYING TO PROTECT THAT WOMAN.
YOU MUST HAVE UPSET GALLADE WHEN YOU PUSHED HER, LOOKER. YOU WERE QUITE RUDE...
MY APOLOGIES. WE HAVE NO INTENTION OF HARMING YOUR TRAINER.
YOU HAVE TO APOLOGIZE TOO, LOOKER!
HMPH.
I'M... SORRY ...
WSSH

WHOA !!
THAT'S BATTLE CASTLE, ONE OF THE BATTLE FACILITIES !!
SHE WENT RIGHT IN WITHOUT WAITING HER TURN IN LINE!!
THAT GALLADE SHE'S GOT WITH HER MUST BE EXTREMELY POWERFUL...!
I BET SHE'S THE FRONTIER BRAIN—THE STRONGEST TRAINER AT BATTLE CASTLE!
SHE DOES LOOK KIND OF MYSTERIOUS ...
MAYBE SHE KNOWS SOME-THING THAT WOULD HELP US.
ALL RIGHT THEN! LET'S BEGIN OUR INVESTIGATION BY TAKING ON THE CHALLENGE OF BATTLE CASTLE!
AGREED!
BUT FIRST... YOU NEED TO GET SOME NEW CLOTHES, LOOKER!

HMPH.
THIS SURE IS A LONG LINE.
YES. A LOT OF TRAINERS ARE HERE TO PAR-TICIPATE.
BUT ACTUALLY...
...THE LINE IS MOVING PRETTY FAST.
PROBABLY BECAUSE MOST OF THE CHALLENGERS LEAVE AFTER GETTING DEFEATED IN THEIR FIRST OR SECOND BATTLE.
SNFFL
SNFFL
MUST BE A TOUGH BATTLE-GROUND.
YES. AND WE'RE ONLY PERMITTED TO FACE THE FRONTIER BRAIN IN THE TWENTY-FIRST BATTLE.
TWENTY-FIRST?!
NEXT CHAL-LENGER, PLEASE!

YOU MUST BE MISS PLATINUM BERLITZ.
THAT'S RIGHT.
WELL THEN, LET'S BEGIN THE FIRST BATTLE— A SINGLE BATTLE USING THREE POKÉMON.
GO !!
BOM

...AND THE CHAL-LENGER WINS!!
HER BATTLE SKILLS ARE PRETTY IMPRES-SIVE.
LADY CAITLIN IS IN A BAD MOOD TODAY...
...BUT THIS WILL SOOTHE HER.
AHA!!
THE FRON-TIER BRAIN!
SO HER NAME IS CAITLIN!
ARE YOU HER VALET OR SOME-THING?

MY APOLOGIES FOR NOT INTRODUCING MYSELF BEFORE.
I AM DARACH ...
...THE FACILITATOR AND JUDGE HERE. PLEASED TO MAKE YOUR ACQUAINTANCE.
HUF
HUF
MY POKÉMON ARE GETTING FATIGUED ALREADY AFTER JUST ONE BATTLE...
HUF
IF ONLY I HAD A BERRY WITH ME...
OH, NOW I REMEMBER!
IN THIS ARENA, I CAN BORROW ITEMS FOR MY POKÉMON, CAN'T I?
DO I NEED TO PAY FOR THEM?
MY WALLET. MY WALLET ...!
HOLD ON...
YES.
WHATEVER YOU DO HERE, YOU'LL NEED CASTLE POINTS FOR.
YOU DON'T RENT ITEMS WITH MONEY HERE. YOU EXCHANGE CASTLE POINTS FOR THEM INSIDE BATTLE CASTLE.
CASTLE POINTS ?

ONE CP* TO GATHER INFORMATION ON YOUR OPPONENT.
TWO CP TO BORROW BERRIES AND ITEMS.
*CASTLE POINT(S)
TEN CP TO HEAL YOUR POKÉMON.
YOU MUST MANAGE YOUR CP WISELY TO MOVE AHEAD IN BATTLE CASTLE.
M-MAN...
...AGE?
NUTS!!
HOW CAN A MILLIONAIRE WHO BUYS RESORT VILLAS WITH A SINGLE SIGNATURE MANAGE THEIR FINANCES?!
I'VE GOT A FEELING WE'RE ALREADY IN BIG TROUBLE!!

Pokémon
Adventures
Adventure 82
Getting the Drop on Gallade I

SMAK
LOPUNNY, DIZZY PUNCH!!
DARACH... REWARD HER WITH CASTLE POINTS.
SET 2 BATTLE 6
TOTAL 13
AND THE CHALLENGER, PLATINUM, WINS THE SIXTH BATTLE OF THE SECOND SET!
YES, MILADY!

MISS PLATINUM, AT LADY CAITLIN'S BEHEST, I WOULD LIKE TO AWARD YOU CASTLE POINTS.
BLIP BLIP
26CP
Add 26 CP
THE BATTLE FRONTIER INSIDE THE BATTLE ZONE...
PLATINUM BERLITZ IS BATTLING INSIDE ONE OF ITS VENUES— THE BATTLE CASTLE!
YOU RECEIVE 10 CP AT THE BEGINNING OF THE CHALLENGE.
AND EVERY TIME YOU WIN A BATTLE, YOU RECEIVE MORE CPS.
YOU WILL CONTINUE TO COLLECT POINTS...
...THAT YOU CAN USE...
...TO HEAL YOUR POKÉMON AND BORROW ITEMS.

SO... HOW ARE YOU GOING TO USE YOUR CP?!
AND ARE YOU GOING TO USE THEM WISELY, MISS PLATINUM?
SHE RECEIVED 26CP, SO NOW PLATINUM HAS 85CP IN ALL!
Platinum
Total: 85 CP
UMM... UHH...
I THINK MAYBE I OUGHT TO USE THE POINTS TO HEAL MY POKÉMON...
BUT IF I USE TOO MANY FOR THAT, I MIGHT NOT HAVE ENOUGH POINTS LEFT TO GATHER INFORMATION ON MY OPPONENTS...
SO MAYBE IT'S BEST FOR ME TO USE THEM TO BORROW BERRIES AND ITEMS ...?
WHAT ARE YOU GOING TO DO, MISS PLATINUM? ARE YOU GOING TO USE YOUR CP? OR SAVE THEM?
HMM!!
USE THEM?! OR SAVE THEM?!
I CAN'T DECIDE WHAT TO USE THEM FOR! SO I GUESS... I'LL JUST SAVE THEM!!

HEH HEH ...
THEN PLEASE MOVE ON TO YOUR NEXT BATTLE.
HER POKÉMON ARE EMPOLEON, RAPIDASH AND LOPUNNY...
ALL FINE POWERFUL POKÉMON!
ADMITTEDLY, HER BATTLE SKILLS ARE NOTEWORTHY.
BUT ONE CANNOT CONQUER THIS CASTLE WITH BATTLE SKILLS ALONE.
HER MANAGEMENT SKILLS MUST BE AS GOOD AS HER BATTLE SKILLS.
BUT IT SEEMS ...
...THIS YOUNG LADY HAS NO MANAGEMENT SKILLS WHATSOEVER. I'LL REPORT TO LADY CAITLIN ABOUT THIS AT ONCE.
AH!!
HE ...
HE NOTICED !!
BOOM
EMPOLEON!!

AQUA JET!!
WOOSH
I... I MISSED!!
RSH RSH RSH
SLASH
CRUSH CLAW!!
CHANGE!!
RAPIDASH!!
BOM

WUUF
AND THE CHAL-LENGER, PLATI-NUM, WINS THE SEVENTH BATTLE OF THE SECOND SET!!
COME HERE FOR A SEC!
PHEW.
NURRRRGH!

LISTEN UP, PLATINUM!
FROM THE LOOK OF THINGS...
...THE KEY TO VICTORY AT BATTLE CASTLE...
...IS USING YOUR CP JUDICIOUSLY.
EMPOLEON'S AQUA JET **MISSED** IN THE LAST BATTLE, REMEMBER?
DO YOU KNOW **WHY**?
BECAUSE THE OPPOSING POKÉMON USED **DETECT**!!
THAT POKÉMON KNEW IN ADVANCE WHAT MOVE YOU WERE GOING TO USE!!
THUNK
EEK!
BUT IF YOU HAD SPENT YOUR CP BEFOREHAND TO GATHER INFORMATION ON YOUR OPPONENT...
Platinum 85CP
Secret Power 20/20
Detect 5/5
Metal Claw 35/35
Slash 20/20
YOU WOULD NEVER HAVE PANICKED LIKE THAT, RIGHT?!
UH-HUH.

COME ON, PLATINUM! USE YOUR CP. YOU HAVE TO MANAGE YOUR CP WISELY, BUT THAT INCLUDES SPENDING THEM!
I'M TRYING ...
BUT...I DON'T KNOW HOW TO CHOOSE HOW MUCH CP TO USE AND FOR WHAT!
I'VE NEVER HAD TO DIVVY UP A LIMITED AMOUNT OF RESOURCES BEFORE...
QUIET !!
I READ EVERY INCH OF THE RULEBOOK WHILE YOU WERE HAVING YOUR POKÉMON BATTLES!!
FAP
LET'S REVIEW IT ONE MORE TIME, SHALL WE?!
TEN CP PER POKÉMON TO HEAL THEM!
EIGHT CP TO HEAL THE POWER POINT OF A MOVE!!
TWO CP EACH TO BORROW A CHERI BERRY, CHESTO BERRY, OR PECHA BERRY!!
ONE CP TO LOOK INSIDE THE POKÉ BALL OF YOUR OPPONENT !!
TWO CP TO CHECK THE STATS AND ABILITY OF THE OPPO- NENT'S POKÉ- MON!!

HUH?
WHAT'S WRONG...?
LOOKER...
I ADMIT THAT I'M BAD AT MANAGING RESOURCES... BUT...
COULD YOU TEACH ME IN A GENTLER MANNER?
WHAT?!
NO ONE HAS EVER SPOKEN SO HARSHLY TO ME BEFORE. NOT MY BUTLER SEBASTIAN OR...
... ANYONE ELSE WHO HAS ASSISTED ME IN THE PAST.
SNORT
OH, OKAY. I'M SORRY. I GUESS I WASN'T CONSIDERING YOUR FEELINGS... I'LL GIVE YOU SOME SPACE.
BUT THINK ABOUT WHAT I SAID!
INTERNATIONAL POLICE EQUIPMENT NO. 5! GALACTICA JET!!
KOFF KOFF

BAM
EYOOp
WHOA !!
POP
WHOA ...
BSS
SNRT
POP
BSS
WHOA ...
BSS
PTT
PTT
I'VE NEVER BEEN GOOD AT TALKING TO PEOPLE! I DON'T KNOW HOW! I ALWAYS FORGET TO CONSIDER THEIR FEELINGS!
THAT WAS THOUGHTLESS OF ME...
SHE'S YOUNG ENOUGH TO BE MY DAUGHTER. I SHOULDN'T HAVE SPOKEN TO HER SO RUDELY.
SIGH ...
I KNOW I HAVE WHAT IT TAKES TO BE BOTH STRONG AND SENSITIVE!
OMMM
OMMM
I CAN'T JUST SHOUT MY IDEAS AT OTHERS!
CALM DOWN, CALM DOWN...
WHAT DID I COME TO THE BATTLE ZONE FOR ANYWAY? AS AN INTERNATIONAL POLICE OFFICER, MY TASK IS TO LEARN ABOUT THE MOVEMENTS OF THAT EVIL ORGANIZATION TEAM GALACTIC!
AND LADY PLATINUM IS SEEKING INFORMATION ABOUT THE DISTORTION WORLD.
THAT'S WHAT WE'RE HERE FOR!! AND WE MUST WORK TOGETHER TO ACCOMPLISH OUR GOALS!!

A SKILLED TRAINER IS BOUND TO HAVE INFORMATION ABOUT THESE THINGS ...
AND IN ORDER TO GET CLOSE TO SKILLED TRAINERS TO QUESTION THEM, WE MUST KEEP WINNING !!
HUH ??
WHERE IS THE ROOM THEY'RE HAVING THEIR POKÉMON BATTLE IN?
IT'S EASY TO GET LOST IN SUCH A BIG PLACE...
HM...
PORTRAITS OF ALL THE CHÂTELAINE AND CHÂTELAINE ANCESTORS ...
THE LORD OF THIS CASTLE, ITS FRONTIER BRAIN, CAITLIN... IS A LADY.
PLATINUM IS A LADY TOO.
THAT MEANS THIS BATTLE WILL BE LADY VERSUS LADY!
IT MIGHT TURN OUT TO BE AN APPROPRIATE MATCH AFTER ALL.
We don't know anything about managing resources...

WHERE IS SHE?! WHERE IS SHE FIGHTING NOW?!
I'D BETTER OBSERVE LADY PLATINUM'S BATTLE CLOSELY!!
THIS IS NO TIME TO THINK NEGATIVE!!
HMPH!!
WHOA!!
ARE YOU IN NEED OF GUIDANCE?
WHAT?!!
THE CHALLENGER, PLATINUM, IS BEFORE THIS VENUE'S FRONTIER BRAIN ALREADY.
SET 3 BATTLE 7
AND SINCE EACH SET CONSISTS OF SEVEN BATTLES...
SHE FACES THE FRONTIER BRAIN ON THE TWENTY-FIRST BATTLE...

THIS IS THE BATTLE AGAINST THE FRONTIER BRAIN!! THAT MEANS...
...CAITLIN IS ON THE BATTLE-FIELD!
WAIT ...
HUH ...?
SHE ISN'T STANDING ON THE BATTLE-FIELD.
WHY NOT ?!
AND IF NOT HER... WHO IS THE FRONTIER BRAIN THAT LADY PLATINUM IS FACING?!
SHALL WE BEGIN ...?
YOUR TWENTY-FIRST BATTLE ...
TUP

...IN THE BATTLE CASTLE!
WHAT?!
THE FRONTIER BRAIN ISN'T THE CHÂTELAINE AT ALL—IT'S HER VALET?!
CORRECT.
LADY CAITLIN IS IN CHARGE, BUT I AM THE FRONTIER BRAIN—THE CASTLE VALET.
I, DARACH...
...AM YOUR OPPONENT!!

BATTLE START !!
LET'S BEGIN !!
HA HA!!
BOM
ROAR
JUMP
PSYCHO CUT!!
GRAB
THAT'S RIGHT, EMPO-LEON!
DID YOU REALLY THINK YOU COULD STOP THIS ATTACK WITH THAT...?
GALLADE!!
NGH NGH

SLASH
GALLADE'S BLADE IS EXPANDABLE!! IT CAN STRETCH OUT **FOREVER**!!
FWOMP
ZOOP
I CAN'T LOSE IN FRONT OF MILADY!!
I SHALL WIN THIS BATTLE, WHAT-EVER IT TAKES!!
WATCH ME, LADY CAITLIN!!

POKéMON
ADVENTURES
Adventure 83
Getting the Drop on Gallade II

FLUMP
EMPO-LEON!!
OOH! I THOUGHT YOU MANAGED TO MOVE BEHIND GALLADE...
BUT THE BLADES ON GALLADE'S ELBOWS WERE EXPAND-ABLE!!
CHANGE PLACES FOR A MOMENT!!
BOM
RAPI-DASH!!
HA HA HA HA!
I'M NOT AS EASY TO BEAT AS YOU THINK!!
KEEP ATTACKING GALLADE!!
PROTECT!!
NEIGH
SWISH
FEINT!!

Platinum's Pokémon

Empoleon (Empoleon, ♀)	Rapidash (Rapidash, ♂)	Lopunny (Lopunny, ♀)
Serious. A little quick tempered. Eats anything.	Modest. Often lost in thought. Favorite flavor is bitter.	Mild. Alert to sounds. Favorite flavor is bitter.
•Type: Water / Steel •Ability: Torrent	•Type: Fire •Ability: Flash Fire	•Type: Normal •Ability: Cute Charm

SNIK
KA-THUD
SNIK
UNABLE TO BATTLE.
YOU MUST HAVE USED PROTECT SO YOUR RAPIDASH WOULDN'T RECEIVE ANY POWERFUL ATTACKS... BUT TOO BAD FOR YOU!
PROTECT AND DETECT HAS NO EFFECT UPON FEINT.
THAT'S ONE DOWN... AND I SUPPOSE I'LL ONLY NEED ANOTHER MINUTE AND A HALF OR SO TO KNOCK OUT YOUR OTHER POKÉMON.
HE'S STRONG!!
DEFINITELY A FRONTIER BRAIN!!
BUT...
I STILL DON'T GET IT!!
WHY IS THE VALET THE FRONTIER BRAIN...
...AND NOT THE CHÂTELAINE?!
I CAN ANSWER YOUR QUESTION.
POINT

MY MIS-TRESS, LADY CAITLIN, HAS INCRED-IBLE POKÉ-MON BATTLE SKILLS.
BUT FOR CERTAIN REASONS, SHE ISN'T ALLOWED TO FIGHT.
THAT'S WHY I STAND IN FOR HER IN BATTLE.
NOW THEN ...
TIME FOR ME TO CALL OUT MY SECOND AND THIRD POKÉMON.
SHOULD I USE STARAPTOR OR HOUN-DOOM...? HM...
AHA HAHA HA!
HEH HEH...
HOUN-DOOM !!
BOM
LOPUNNY !!
BOM
TUK
TUK
TUK
TUK
TUK

I HAD BETTER ATTACK ITS WEAK POINT!!
FOOM
FOCUS BLAST !!
NICE MOVE. FOCUS BLAST IS A FIGHTING-TYPE MOVE, WHICH IS A DARK-TYPE POKÉMON'S WEAKNESS.
BUT ...
TINK
GASP
TIME TO RETALIATE, HOUN-DOOM!!
GASP
FIRE FANG !!
A FOCUS SASH!!
EXACTLY!
AN ITEM WHICH PROTECTS A POKÉ-MON FROM FAINTING WHEN HIT BY A KNOCK-OUT MOVE!!

BOM
YOU'VE SWITCHED TO EMPO-LEON AGAIN.
HYDRO PUMP!!
UNABLE TO BAT-TLE.
EXCELLENT!!

DARACH'S THIRD POKÉMON!!
BUT...
... EMPOLEON'S ICE MOVES HAVE AN ADVANTAGE OVER IT!!
BOM
STARAPTOR!!
BLIZZARD!!
FOOOSH
FWEF FWEF FWEF
IT'S DOUBLE TEAM! YOU'RE NOT GOING TO BE ABLE TO HIT ME **THAT** EASILY!!
EVEN IF YOU MANAGE TO GRAZE IT...
...IT CAN HEAL ITSELF WITH ROOST!!
ALL RIGHT, BUT ...

...I'LL GIVE IT A TRY!!
SNK
AND I'LL TRY!!
AND TRY AGAIN !!
UNABLE TO BATTLE.
YOU MANAGED TO HOLD OUT!! ONE MORE TO GO!!
IT LOOKS LIKE YOU REALLY WANT TO...
...DRAG MY LAST POKÉ-MON OUT INTO THE FRAY!!
HAR HAR !!
BOM
BOM

SHE HAS TWO LEFT, YES, BUT THEY'RE BOTH OUT OF BREATH AND WEAK!!
AND MY GALLADE IS PRETTY MUCH UNDAMAGED!!
YOU OUTNUMBER HIM!!
KLNK KLNK
THAT'S **HIS** LAST POKÉMON, BUT YOU STILL HAVE TWO LEFT!!
RELAX, PLATINUM!!
NUMBERS ARE OF NO IMPORTANCE HERE!!
NIGHT SLASH!!
SLASH
HE'S... ...STRONG!!

YOU MUSTN'T GIVE UP, PLATINUM!!
IF YOU GIVE UP OR LOSE, WE'LL GET THROWN OUT OF HERE!!
AND THAT MEANS WE'LL LOSE THE OPPORTUNITY TO GATHER INFORMATION FROM DARACH AND CAITLIN!!
ON THE OTHER HAND, IF YOU WIN, WE GET TO TALK WITH THE FRONTIER BRAIN!
YOU **HAVE** TO WIN. IT'S THE ONLY WAY FOR US TO...
...GET WHAT WE CAME HERE FOR!!
HMM?
HUF.
HUF.
FSSH
GASP!
GASP!
FSSH
GASP!
FSSH
UGGH
PLINK...

KERFLUMP
HA HA HA HA HA!!
YOU DON'T EVEN HAVE ENOUGH STRENGTH TO PUNCH ANYMORE!!
PAN!!
BOM
PAN!!
THE ONLY ONE LEFT IS YOUR GOOD-AS-FINISHED EMPOLEON!!
THE END RESULT IS A FOREGONE CONCLUSION!!
GALLADE... FINISH EMPOLEON OFF!!
SHF
SHF
SLASH
STAB

HEY!!
NOW'S YOUR CHANCE, EMPO-LEON!!
4B
OH!
WHAT?!
DRILL PECK!!
BZZBZZBZ

AAAAAARGH!!
UNABLE TO BATTLE.
CHAL-LENGER WINS.
I WON!
SLUMP
WELL DONE, PLATI-NUM!!
UM... SO WHAT EX-ACTLY HAP-PENED AT THE END THERE?
LOPUN-NY'S ABILITY IS...
...CUTE CHARM, RIGHT?
GALLADE ATTACKED LOPUNNY WITH NIGHT SLASH—WHICH IS A DIRECT ATTACK—SO THE MOMENT IT TOUCHED LOPUNNY'S BODY IT GOT INFATUATED.
IN OTHER WORDS, GALLADE HAD FEELINGS THAT MADE IT HARD FOR IT TO ATTACK LOPUNNY.
I GUESS THERE'S NO WAY THAT COULD BE HELPED...
...BUT IT WAS ENTIRELY DARACH'S MISTAKE TO LEAVE AN OPENING FOR LOPUNNY TO ATTACK WITH DIZZY PUNCH, WHICH CAUSES CONFUSE.
CON-FUSE! OF COURSE!
THAT'S WHY GALLADE ATTACKED ITSELF!!
AND IT WAS ALL THANKS TO YOU, LOOKER!
I FOLLOWED YOUR ADVICE AND USED MY CP TO GATHER ALL THE INFORMATION I COULD!
OH MY!!

MANAGING RESOURCES IS FUN!!
I'M SLOWLY FIGURING OUT HOW TO MANAGE MY CP... ONCE I DECIDED TO BORROW ITEMS AND SET A GOAL IT GOT EASIER.
270CP !!
FOCUS SASH—EVEN THOUGH I HAD TO USE MORE THAN 270CP FOR IT!
I BORROWED AN ITEM TOO.
IF YOU KNOW THE ENEMY AND KNOW YOURSELF, YOU NEED NOT FEAR A HUNDRED BATTLES !!
AND NOW TO RECOGNIZE YOUR GREAT SKILL WE PRESENT YOU WITH...
I'M SO ASHAMED.
YOU LOST BECAUSE YOU UNDERESTIMATED YOUR OPPONENT. YOU ASSUMED SHE WOULDN'T LEARN HOW TO MANAGE HER CP. LET THIS BE A LESSON TO YOU.
HMPH.
I LOST... AND IN FRONT OF LADY CAITLIN TOO...
I AM DEFEATED.
...A COMMEMORATIVE PRINT.
ALL THE TRAINERS WHO DEFEAT THE FRONTIER BRAIN COLLECT THEM.
AS PROOF OF YOUR VICTORIES AT EACH OF THE BATTLE FRONTIER FACILITIES.
THAT'S RIGHT.
A... COMMEMORATIVE PRINT?

THANK YOU VERY MUCH! BUT...WHERE SHOULD I KEEP IT?
OH!! I'VE GOT A SOLUTION READY RIGHT HERE!!
INTERNATIONAL POLICE EQUIPMENT NO. 6!!
VS RECORDER!!
ER... EVERY CHALLENGER WHO TAKES PART IN THE BATTLE FRONTIER GETS ONE OF THOSE...
Ah-hem...
OH. I GUESS SAYING THAT HAS GOTTEN TO BE A HABIT EVERY TIME I PULL SOMETHING OUT OF MY POCKET...
OKAY. STICK THAT...
...RIGHT **HERE.**
AND NOW, PLATINUM...THE MOMENT WE'VE BEEN WAITING FOR!
YOU'RE THE WINNER, SO THERE'S NO NEED TO HOLD BACK!
ASK FOR THE INFORMATION WE SEEK.
OH, YES!
INFORMATION...?
YES. FULL DISCLOSURE, I'M AN INVESTIGATOR FOR THE INTERNATIONAL POLICE.
I HAVE TWO QUESTIONS FOR YOU.
FIRST, WHAT DO YOU KNOW ABOUT THE DISTORTION WORLD?
SECOND...

WHAT CAN YOU TELL US ABOUT TEAM GALACTIC?
WE KNOW THEY'RE BAD PEOPLE AND THEY MIGHT BE HIDING OUT HERE AT THE BATTLE ZONE.
WE'D LIKE TO KNOW MORE!
HM... I DON'T KNOW ANYTHING ABOUT THE DISTORTION WORLD. BUT I DO KNOW SOMETHING ABOUT THIS GROUP...
YOU DO?!
YES. THERE HAVE BEEN RUMORS OF SIGHTINGS OF THESE PEOPLE AROUND HERE RECENTLY.
I THINK IT WAS... NEAR STARK MOUNTAIN...
HOLD IT RIGHT THERE!!
STEP
IF IT'S INTEL ON THAT MOUNTAIN YOU'RE LOOKING FOR...
...I'VE GOT PLENTY FOR YOU!!
AHA HA HA!

Pokémon Adventures
Adventure 84 Clobbering Claydol

JUMP
PLUNK
IF IT'S...
STARK MOUNTAIN YOU'RE TALKING ABOUT...
...THEN YOU'RE ...
...TALKING ABOUT HEATRAN, AREN'T YOU?
I'LL TELL YOU ALL ABOUT IT!
HEH HEH ...

STARK MOUNTAIN ...? HEATRAN ...? WHA...?
WHAT ARE YOU TALKING ABOUT?!
AND WHO ARE YOU ANYWAY?
THE NAME'S BUCK!
WELL?
DON'T YOU REMEMBER ME?! DON'T TELL ME YOU'VE FORGOTTEN ALREADY!
HUH?
HM...
AGH!!
THE GUY FROM THE BATTLEGROUND?!
LOOKER, DO YOU KNOW THIS YOUNG MAN?
OH YEAH!
YOU BEAT THE FRONTIER BRAIN JUST NOW, DIDN'T YOU?
HOW MANY COMMEMORATIVE PRINTS HAVE YOU GOT?
HMM, JUST ONE!
WHAT'S YOUR NAME?
GRAB

YOU HAND THAT BACK THIS MINUTE! I DON'T HAVE TO TELL YOU ANYTHING!!
GRAB
UM...
EXCUSE ME...
MY NAME IS PLATINUM...
PLATINUM BERLITZ.
OH ...?
WHAT ARE YOU DOING HERE, BUCK?
ISN'T IT OBVIOUS, DARACH? I CAME TO TALK TO THIS MAN!
HEY! LET GO OF ME!
YESTERDAY, HE SNUCK INTO THE BATTLEGROUND—WHICH I'M IN CHARGE OF!
AND WHEN I QUESTIONED HIM, HE RAN OFF.
HEY!!
HM...
I SPENT THE WHOLE DAY LOOKING FOR HIM—AND NOW I'VE FINALLY FOUND HIM!
AND THEN I OVERHEARD YOU GUYS TALKING ABOUT STARK MOUNTAIN.
SO I COULDN'T HELP MYSELF.

DO YOU KNOW ABOUT THESE PEOPLE, BUCK? THE ONES SEEN HANGING AROUND STARK MOUNTAIN?
YEAH. I'VE DONE SOME RESEARCH ON THEM MYSELF.
THEY'RE A REALLY BIG GROUP. AND THEY'RE CRAWLING ALL OVER THAT MOUNTAIN!
WHICH MEANS...
...THEY MUST BE AFTER SOMETHING BIG INSIDE THE MOUNTAIN.
INSIDE... THE MOUNTAIN?
TO PUT IT SIMPLY—IT'S A CAVE.
STARK MOUNTAIN IS A VOLCANO.
IT'S RIDDLED WITH MAZE-LIKE CAVES.
AND IT'S SAID THAT THE LORD OF STARK MOUNTAIN LIVES IN THE BOTTOMMOST CAVE.
I'M THINKING THOSE PEOPLE ARE AFTER THE POKÉMON HEATRAN!

IT'S A SUPER POWERFUL POKÉMON—THE LAVA DOME POKÉMON.
ACCORDING TO LEGEND, HEATRAN'S MAGMA STORM TRAPS ITS ENEMY INSIDE A FIRESTORM!
I SEE.
I GET IT.
THANK YOU FOR THIS VALUABLE INFORMATION.
I'LL TAKE OVER FROM HERE. NOW GUIDE ME TO STARK MOUNTAIN, PRONTO!
NO WAY!
WHAT ?!
I DON'T MIND GIVING YOU INFO OR TELLING YOU ABOUT IT...
... BUT ...
...I DON'T WANT YOU SNOOPIN' AROUND MY TERRITORY!!
I'LL TAKE THAT PHOTO, THANK YOU!!
GRAB

I'M GONNA ...
...TAKE CARE OF THESE GUYS MYSELF!!
WHAT ARE YOU TALKING ABOUT ?!
I'M AN INTERNATIONAL POLICE OFFICER !!
ALL THE MORE REASON FOR ME TO HANDLE THIS.
I DON'T LIKE COPS. THEY'RE SO FULL OF THEMSELVES!
DOINK
KRASH
SEE YA!
TELEPORT!!

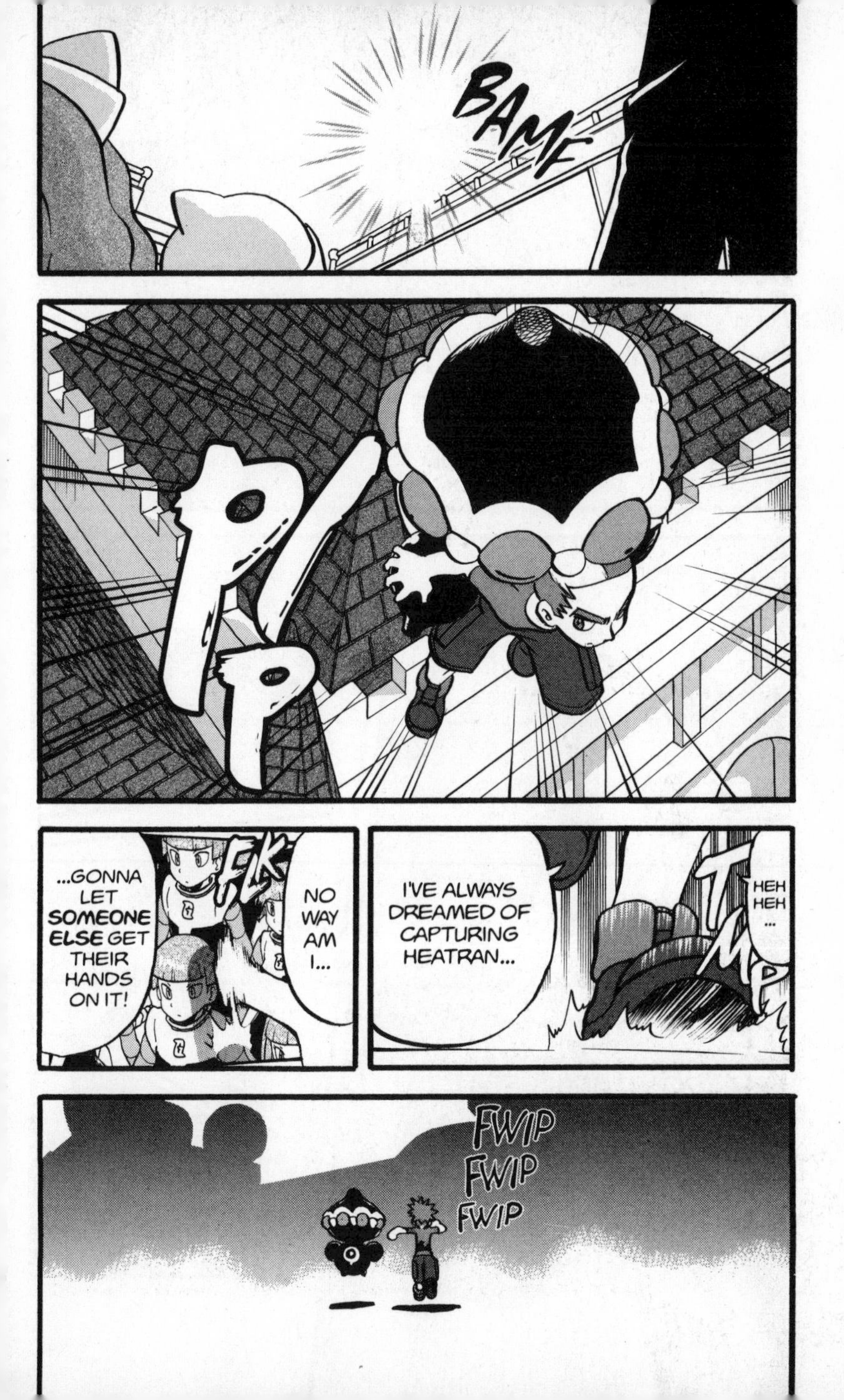
BAMF
POP
NO WAY AM I...
...GONNA LET SOMEONE ELSE GET THEIR HANDS ON IT!
FLK
HEH HEH ...
I'VE ALWAYS DREAMED OF CAPTURING HEATRAN...
TMP
FWIP
FWIP
FWIP

HMM ...
IT WAS SUCH A TRIUMPH FOR YOU TO EMERGE VICTORIOUS FROM BATTLE CASTLE!
AND NOW BUCK HAS KIND OF RAINED ON YOUR PARADE...
YES, WELL ...
HMPH. WHAT A BRAT!
IT SEEMED LIKE HE KNEW DARACH, DIDN'T IT...?
A LITTLE BROTHER... OF THE ELITE FOUR...
THE FRONTIER BRAINS...
THE GYM LEADERS...
MAYBE THERE'S A LINK, SOME SORT OF CONNECTION, BETWEEN ALL THOSE SKILLED TRAINERS...
COME TO THINK OF IT, THE FIRST DAY I MET HIM...
...HE TOLD ME HE WAS THE YOUNGER SIBLING OF ONE OF THE ELITE FOUR.
MY BIG BROTHER IS ONE OF THE ELITE FOUR, YOU KNOW!! DON'T MAKE ME GO AND CALL HIM!

WE HAVE TO KEEP OUR FOCUS ON THE ENEMY!!
ESPECIALLY IF THEY'RE MAKING THEIR MOVE...
...AS A COORDINATED TEAM... WITH THEIR COORDINATED HIP HAIRSTYLES AND UNIFORMS...
UH... YES.
WHAT SHOULD WE DO NOW, LOOKER?
ABOUT TEAM GALACTIC, I MEAN.
THAT'S A DIFFICULT QUESTION, PLATINUM...
I MANAGED TO GET SOME INTEL ABOUT TEAM GALACTIC.
BUT UNFORTUNATELY...
WE DIDN'T GET ANY INTEL ABOUT THE DISTORTION WORLD.
DO YOU WANT TO CONTINUE TAKING ON THE BATTLE CHALLENGES SO AS TO GATHER MORE INFORMATION FROM OTHER FRONTIER BRAINS?
YES!
THEN WE'D BETTER CONCENTRATE ON THAT FOR THE TIME BEING...
FWMP

I GOT AHOLD OF A MAP SO I KNOW WHERE STARK MOUNTAIN IS.
IT WON'T BE A PROBLEM FOR ME TO GET THERE.
BUT I'M WORRIED I'LL END UP IN A FIGHT WITH THAT BRAT...
AND IT WOULD BE TOO DANGEROUS FOR ME TO COME FACE TO FACE WITH TEAM GALACTIC ALL BY MYSELF.
WELL, FOR NOW, LET'S CALL IT A DAY...
I'LL SHOW YOU TO THE GUEST-ROOM...
FFT
DON'T WORRY ABOUT ME.
YOU'D BETTER GET SOME REST TO PREPARE FOR TOMORROW!
GOOD NIGHT!
INTERNATIONAL POLICE EQUIPMENT NO. 7!!
HYPER COMPACT ONE-TOUCH TENT!!
POP
NOW THEN, TIME TO WRITE MY REPORT...

CHRP
CHRP
HM?
OH NO!! I OVER-SLEPT!! THE SUN IS HIGH ALREADY!!
PLATI-NUM!! HEY, PLATI-NUM!!

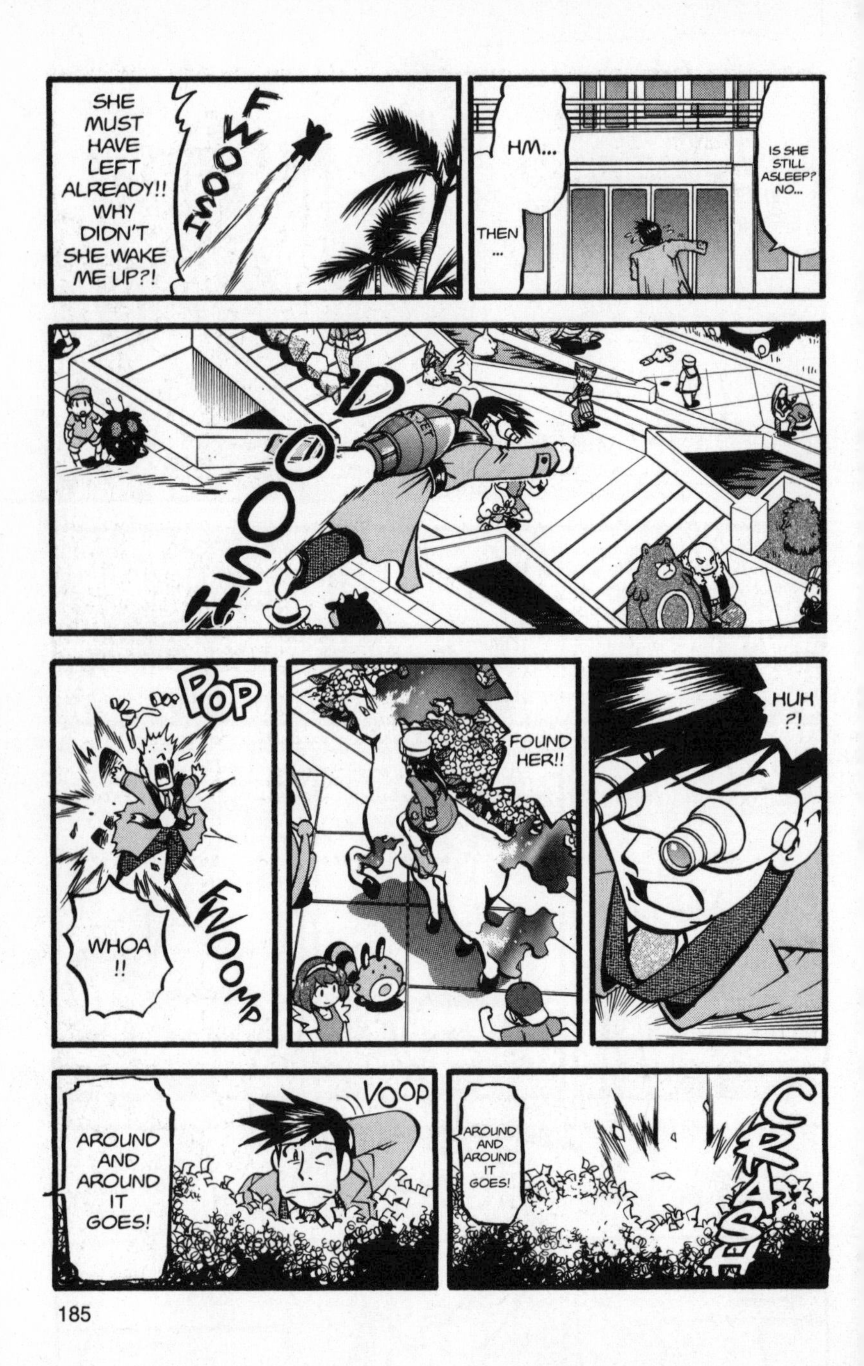
IS SHE STILL ASLEEP? NO...
HM...
THEN ...
FWOOSH
SHE MUST HAVE LEFT ALREADY!! WHY DIDN'T SHE WAKE ME UP?!
DOOOSH
HUH ?!
FOUND HER!!
POP
WHOA !!
FWOOMP
CRASH
AROUND AND AROUND IT GOES!
VOOP
AROUND AND AROUND IT GOES!

AROUND AND AROUND IT GOES!
BATTLE ARCADE!
THE WHEEL IS SPINNING!!
PLATI-NUM?
AH!!
I'M SORRY, LOOKER!
I HEARD THIS DELIGHTFUL SONG WHEN I WOKE UP, SO I...
AROUND AND AROUND IT GOES!
SONG...? YOU MEAN... THAT CARNIVAL BARKER'S CHANT?
AROUND AND AROUND IT GOES!
WHY, YES...
YOU LIKE PLAYING ROULETTE AND WHAT-NOT?
AROUND AND AROUND IT GOES!
YES, I DO.
HM...
AROUND AND AROUND IT GOES!
WELL, FROM THE LOOK OF THINGS...
...THE SECOND CHALLENGE YOU'RE GOING FOR IS...

...THIS ONE...
...THE BATTLE ARCADE!!
STEP RIGHT UP, STEP RIGHT UP! IF YOU'RE A CHALLENGER, PLEASE GO RIGHT INSIDE!!
WE GOT IN? JUST LIKE THAT? WITHOUT WAITING?
THIS SURE IS DIFFERENT FROM THE BATTLE CASTLE! WE HAD TO WAIT IN LINE FOR **AGES** THERE.
THEY EVEN NEED A BARKER TO LURE IN CHALLENGERS...
THAT MUST MEAN THIS CHALLENGE IS **VERY UNPOPULAR.**
WRONG.
WHOA!!

YOU AGAIN!
THE REASON THERE AREN'T ANY CHALLENGERS HERE IS NOT BECAUSE THIS FACILITY IS UNPOPULAR.
IT IS BECAUSE ...
...THIS CHALLENGE IS VERY DIFFICULT.
DEFEATING THE ARCADE STAR...
...IS VERY, VERY, VERY DIFFICULT.
ROUTE 227
HUF.
HUF.
HUF HUF
THE MOUNTAIN SURFACE HERE IS ROUGH.
BUT I CAN'T GET TO STARK MOUNTAIN IF I DON'T CROSS THIS TERRAIN SOMEHOW...
GASP.
C'MON, LET'S GO!!

CONTINUE TO FOLLOW HIS MOVEMENTS.
VERY WELL ...
HM... HM... I SEE...
A CHILD HAS BEEN STICKING HIS NOSE INTO OUR BUSINESS... AND HE'S HEADING HERE NOW?
THUD
RMBL RMBL RMBL RMBL

Adventure 85
Interrupting Ivysaur
Pokémon Adventures

1.
2.
3.
ROU-LETTE WHEEL ...
... SPIN !!
SPIN
DINK DINK DINK DINK DINK DINK
KLK

THERE IT GOES!! THE EVENT FOR THIS BATTLE IS...
BOOMP
BLACK PANEL. BERRY MARK.
...THE BLACK FIELD!!
AND PLATINUM'S POKÉMON ...
...WILL RECEIVE A SITRUS BERRY BEFORE THE BATTLE BEGINS!!
FLOOP
FLOOP
FLOOP

THE VETRAN TRAINER IN THE RED FIELD IS BECK...
...AND ALL THREE OF HIS POKÉMON ARE NO LONGER ABLE TO BATTLE.
THEREFORE, PLATINUM BERLITZ, IN THE BLACK FIELD, WINS!!
WELL DONE!! YOUR OPPONENT WAS A VETERAN TRAINER, SO THERE WERE TIMES WHEN YOU WERE IN DANGER OF LOSING, BUT...
...I WAS ABLE TO HEAL MY POKÉMON SINCE I RECEIVED THOSE BERRIES.
IT'S ALL THANKS TO THE LUCK OF THE WHEEL!
ARE YOU GOING TO CON-TINUE? OR QUIT?
I'LL CON-TINUE!!
THE CHALLENGE CONTINUES!! NEXT CHALLENGER, COME OUT!!
LEONARDO, THE POKÉMON BREEDER !!

ROU-LETTE WHEEL ... SPIN!!
SPIN
DINK
DINK
DINK
DINK
+Lv
PUSH
AND... STOP.
THE PANEL HAS A SUNNY MARK.
THE BATTLE WILL TAKE PLACE IN SUNNY WEATHER!!
BWAM
ROAR
PLATI-NUM'S SECOND CHAL-LENGE IN THE BATTLE FRON-TIER...
...IS THE BATTLE ARCADE.

THERE ARE VARIOUS TYPES OF EVENTS.
A SPIN OF THE WHEEL DETERMINES THE LOCATION OF THE BATTLE AND THE CIRCUMSTANCES.
FOR EXAMPLE, A WEATHER PANEL ...
BATTLE IN RAINY WEATHER
AND STATUS AIL-MENTS LIKE...
... POI-SON OR PARA-LYZE ...
POISONS OR PARALYZES THE POKÉMON
OR THE POKÉ-MON GET BERRIES ...
POKÉMON RECEIVE BERRIES
FIRE BLAST !!
PLATINUM BERLITZ WINS!!
YAY !!

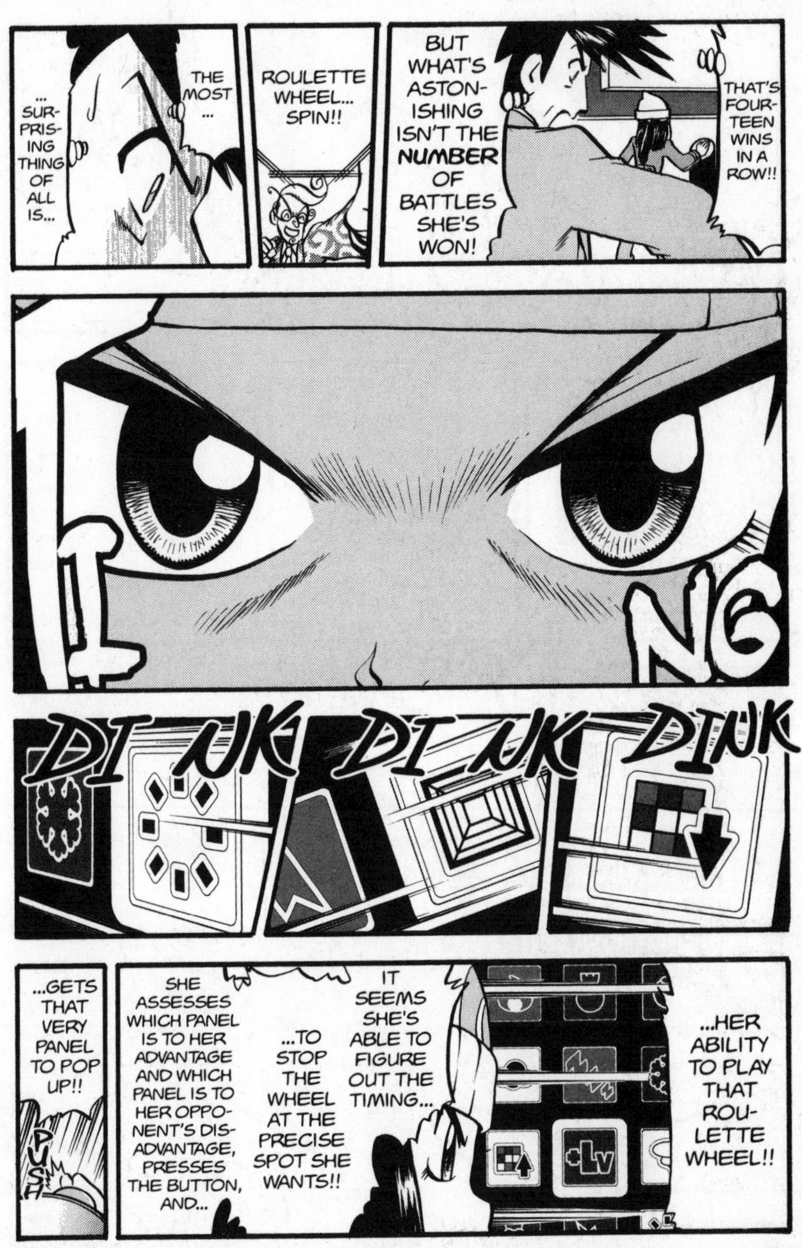
THAT'S FOURTEEN WINS IN A ROW!!
BUT WHAT'S ASTONISHING ISN'T THE NUMBER OF BATTLES SHE'S WON!
ROULETTE WHEEL... SPIN!!
THE MOST ...
... SURPRISING THING OF ALL IS...
NG
DINK DINK DINK
...HER ABILITY TO PLAY THAT ROULETTE WHEEL!!
IT SEEMS SHE'S ABLE TO FIGURE OUT THE TIMING...
...TO STOP THE WHEEL AT THE PRECISE SPOT SHE WANTS!!
SHE ASSESSES WHICH PANEL IS TO HER ADVANTAGE AND WHICH PANEL IS TO HER OPPONENT'S DISADVANTAGE, PRESSES THE BUTTON, AND...
PUSH
...GETS THAT VERY PANEL TO POP UP!!

CHH CHH CHH
BOMP
8
THIS BATTLE WILL TAKE PLACE IN A HAIL-STORM!!
SHE TOLD ME SHE ENJOYED THIS TYPE OF THING...
CHHH CHH
INTERNAT
NO WONDER SHE GOT LURED IN TO THIS CHAL-LENGE SO QUICKLY BY THIS BARKER.
AS LONG AS SHE CONTINUES TO WIN, SHE GETS TO DECIDE WHEN TO STOP THE ROULETTE.
CHHH CHHH
AT THIS RATE ...!!
QUE SERA, SERA.
TIP
TIP
LIFE IS LIKE A SPINNING ROULETTE WHEEL.
HEY! IS IT TRUE THAT WE'VE GOT AN AMAZINGLY TALENTED CHALLENGER TODAY?!
OOH!! SEVEN-TEEN WINS IN A ROW!!

SHE'S ALMOST THERE!
OOOH!! ARCADE STAR...
...DAHLIA!!
I WILL ACCEPT AND FACE THE CHALLENGER FOR...
...THE TWENTY-FIRST BATTLE!
SHE MUST BE...
...THE FRONTIER BRAIN OF THIS VENUE!!
TRYING TO BEAT THE ARCADE STAR...
...IS VERY, VERY, VERY DIFFI-CULT!!
SHE IS A FORMI-DABLE OPPO-NENT.
WHICH MEANS...
...THERE'S A GOOD POSSIBILITY SHE MIGHT KNOW SOMETHING OF USE TO ME...
...ABOUT THE DIS-TORTION WORLD!

THE ONLY OPPORTUNITY WE'LL GET TO TALK WITH HER IS WHEN I WIN AND RECEIVE THE COMMEMORATIVE PRINT!
SO WE **HAVE** TO WIN THIS BATTLE—NO MATTER WHAT!
ISN'T THAT RIGHT, RAPIDASH?!
LOPUNNY?!
EMPOLEON?!
HERE WE ARE...
RMBL RMBL RMBL
THE ENTRANCE TO THE TUNNEL THAT LEADS INTO THE CAVES OF STARK MOUNTAIN!
I'VE PLAYED HERE SINCE I WAS A KID...
...BUT I'VE NEVER COME **THIS** FAR.
I MIGHT NOT GET CELL PHONE RECEPTION INSIDE THE CAVE...
...SO I'D BETTER CALL HIM NOW!
RING RING

FLINT SPEAKING.
IT'S ME—BUCK!!
HEY, BUCK! I WAS JUST THINKING OF CALLING YOU!
FROM THE SOUND OF THINGS, YOU'RE AT THE MOUNTAIN, AREN'T YOU?
BINGO!!
YOU'VE BEEN TALKING SO MUCH ABOUT IT, I DECIDED TO INVESTIGATE THAT MOUNTAIN MYSELF.
I FOUND OUT THERE'S SOME KIND OF TREASURE INSIDE IT—JUST THE KIND OF THING THOSE BAD GUYS WOULD BE AFTER.
TREASURE?!
THAT'S RIGHT! IT'S CALLED...
...THE MAGMA STONE.
APPARENTLY, IT'S A STONE THAT CONTAINS INCREDIBLE POWER. IT'S LOCATED IN THE INNERMOST AREA OF THE VOLCANO.
THOSE GUYS IN THE FANCY UNIFORMS YOU SAW ARE...
HUH?
HELLO? HELLO-O-O-?
RMBL

I GUESS I'M OUT OF RANGE? THE CONNECTION BROKE...
HMM, A TREASURE...
MAYBE I WAS WRONG...
I WAS SURE THOSE BAD GUYS WERE AFTER HEATRAN...
BUT MAYBE THEY'RE AFTER THAT TREASURE INSTEAD!
WELL...
...THE QUICKEST WAY TO FIND OUT IS TO JUST...
...ASK THEM IN PERSON.
I KNOW YOU'VE BEEN FOLLOWING ME!!
COME OUT!
YOU WANNA PIECE OF ME?! HUH?!
HM...
CLAYDOL, SANDSTORM!!
WOOOSH

BOING
NOW TELL ME!!
WHAT ARE YOU GUYS AFTER ?!
AND WHY ARE YOU TAILING ME?!
SMAK
WHY WON'T YOU ...
... SAY SOME-THING ?!
SMAK

HUF
HUF
TCH!
I'M GET-TING NO-WHERE FAST.
CLAYDOL, WE'RE GONNA KEEP GOING NONSTOP UNTIL WE GET THAT TREASURE!
IF THEY'RE AFTER THIS MAGMA STONE...
...WE NEED TO GET TO IT AND PROTECT IT BEFORE THEY CAN GET THEIR GRUBBY PAWS ON IT!
GO!!
FWIP

USE YOUR POWER ...
...TO FIND THE WAY THERE !!
HA! I'VE LOST THEM!
WHAT'S THE MAT-TER ...?
LOOK, WE'VE FOUND IT!
THE MAGMA STONE!
TO BE CONTINUED...

Message from
Hidenori Kusaka

My current goal is to climb the stairs to the editorial floor whenever I drop by the offices of Shogakukan, our publisher. The editorial office is on the seventh floor, so I'm pretty much out of breath by the time I get there. It's a good thing it's on the seventh floor, since I probably wouldn't even attempt the climb if it was on the eighth. The number is just right. In fact, it's perfect! The other editorial office is on the sixth floor, which is a little easier...!

Message from
Satoshi Yamamoto

When we began the Diamond and Pearl/Platinum story arc, we decided not to give the main characters any superhuman qualities. Now the story is coming to an end. However, Platinum is super wealthy and Pearl has a special ability to predict a Pokémon's next move. It's always been a challenge for me to draw Dia as a main character since he's so...normal. I had a lot of difficulty with his facial expressions, his movements and even just drawing his lines. And now he's become my favorite character.

More Adventures Coming Soon...

Lady faces two new Pokémon Battle challenges when she must swap her Pokémon with her opponent and fight with rented Pokémon! Then the arena for her next challenge, the Battle Frontier, begins to suffer from a mysterious malfunction... Who is using technology to control Pokémon instead of building a trusting relationship with them?!

Meanwhile, will Dia and Pearl find the Legendary Pokémon of the Sinnoh region—before it's too late?

Plus, say hello to Togekiss, Empoleon, Heatran, Kakuna, Seedot, Ledian, Dragonite, and Rotom!

AVAILABLE FEBRUARY 2014!

THIS IS THE END OF THIS GRAPHIC NOVEL!

To properly enjoy this VIZ Media graphic novel, please turn it around and begin reading from right to left.

This book has been printed in the original Japanese format in order to preserve the orientation of the original artwork. Have fun with it!

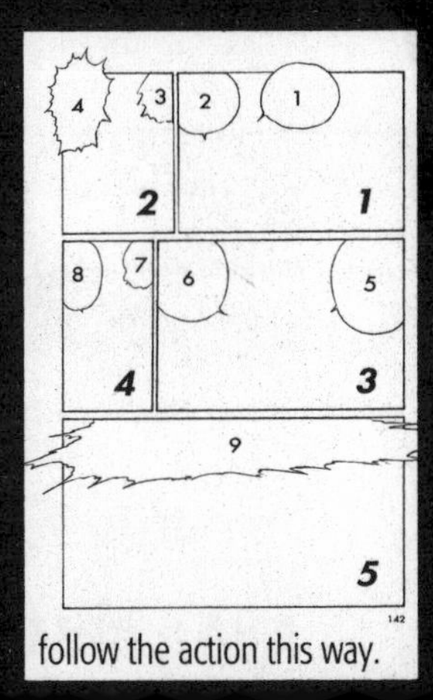